The Adventures
of

Eli Benjamin Bear

in

"A Heart's Journey Home"

Written by
Hal Price

Illustrations by Michael Bayouth

TABLE OF CONTENTS

I

"It's Your Bedtime"

You're safe and warm, the day is done.
Your nighttime journey starts.
Our dreamlike silence opens space
To invite words from our hearts.

Our words can paint a picture
That moves through space and time.
I now will take you to a place
To meet dear friends of mine.

My home is small and simple
With mountains green and tall.
The waterfalls are crystal clear,
Our worries there are small.

There's a towering wooden statue there
That is honored by each bear,
She's a maiden Indian princess
Who looks over us with care.

My home is truly magical
The bears in my town sing,
They're kind to one another
They feel blessed by everything.

The bears there told me, "Hearts have wings
They can take us anywhere.
Imagination is the key,
We are not your average bear!"

Our words and minds can carry us
To places far and wide.
I want you now to hop on board
To take my magic ride!

First rest your eyes and hear your breath.
This silence makes you still.
Then listen to your beating heart
And how it makes you feel.

You now are ready for your trip.
I'm glad that you are here.
I've invited LOVE to sit with us.
So, the world can disappear.

2

Welcome to the World
Elijah Benjamin Bear

I experienced first a blinding light
Muffled noises filled the air,
My first breath was a giant gasp
Slimy Goo was in my hair!

The commotion felt like panic.
I felt hands comfort me.
I was lifted from the leafy ground,
I was confined, but now set free.

Everything was very blurry.
I tried to make a sound,
But my voice was weak and helpless.
There were strangers all around.

I arrived two months too early
While my mom worked in our yard.
It was not the way she planned it,
But change comes without regard.

Our neighbors rushed to help us
And my grandmothers ran up too!
They lifted mom up off the ground
And asked what they could do.

Mom said, "Get me to Urgent Care!
Can you carry me to town?
Let's get to Bear Memorial
Before the sun goes down."

Mom said, "His heart seems very weak.
Can we please pick up our pace?"
My Uncle said, "I'll run ahead
To alert the nurses we'll need space!"

As we walked the streets of Cooper Springs
I was taking all this in,
Then one lady counted up my toes
And said, "Yes, Ruth, he has all ten!"

My grandma, Nina, came with us
Dad's mom was right behind.
We marched to Bear Memorial
With our relatives all in line!

The year was 1955.
It was just before the winter.
It happened truly all so fast.
That I really don't remember!

Mom was carried by two grizzly bears
I was nestled in her arms.
They were running up the mountainside
Blowing whistles and alarms.

I thought, "Wow! I must be special!"
They're all making such a fuss.
I really love this grand parade
But we could have rode the bus!

Some grey old bear then pinched my cheeks.
Saying, "He's hairy like his dad!
Ruth, where is Pete, he should be here?
I know he will be glad!"

Mom said, "Pete's in Atlanta now
He'll be gone for three more weeks.
He's selling Honey-Beary Jam.
This is when his sales all peak!"

I heard mom say, "Please let Pete know!
And tell him to come home.
I need him here in Bear Ridge now,
I can't do this alone!"

To get my Dad was some ordeal
And this task could cause great pains!
(Because there were no cell phones then, and
Bears weren't allowed on planes)!

Dad's mother, Leila, said she'd wire
A note by Western Union,
And pray that this would reach her son
To complete this new reunion.

We stormed into the hospital
There were 15 in our posse.
Everyone was loudly trying to help
And the ladies all were bossy!

The nurse said, "Please give us some room
We need to get the mother.
We'll check her in, who's next of kin?
So, ya'll just chat with one another!"

The nurses put my mom and me
Into a chair with wheels.
We rode around so very fast
It was an awesome thrill!

We finally found a bright white room
With metal stuff around.
Mom asked me please to go to sleep
So we both could settle down!

In our quiet moment all alone,
Mom said, "I'll name you now.
Your dad and I picked out your name
And we both agreed somehow.

She said, "We'll call you Eli Bear,
But that's your simple name.
Your given name 'Elijah'
Will provide you quiet acclaim.

"Elijah Benjamin Bear you are!
Your father will be proud.
You'll make a difference in this world!"
(She solemnly avowed.)

That name then settled in my soul.
It felt like it was me.
And I knew then from that day on,
I'd be who I must be.

3
THE DOCTOR'S RECOMMENDATION

The doctors came to check me out.
They put sensors on my chest.
They told me it might take a while,
So we should get some rest.

As we waited on the tests to run
Mom looked at me and said,
"Hang in there, child, we'll get through this
Just rest your little head."

We waited ninety minutes
For the doctors to reveal
The findings of their studies
And just what I had to heal.

The doctors said my heart was weak.
Mom hurt to hear this truth.
"We hate to break this news to you
But you must know this, Ruth."

"Your child came way too early!"
The doctor quickly warned.
"His heart needs help and right away.
It has not fully formed.

"We're not equipped to help him here,"
These words I now recall.
"This sweet cub now needs special care,
To grow up strong and tall."

The doctors all agreed it best
To send me out-of-state.
Mom pulled me toward her chest and asked,
"Are you sure there's no mistake?"

"We're certain Ma'am, we've all reviewed
His X-rays and his charts.
Your son was born with some defect.
We need to fix his heart.

"We will take him to Heroic Hearts.
They have a special wing,
They care for kids and infants, too.
Hearts are their special thing.

"It's in a town called Duck Bill,
Where each surgeon is quite smart.
Their nurses spend three days a week
Teaching kids about their heart.

"It is 600 miles from here.
The rains make all roads "slippy."
We will drive Eli for half the night
To arrive in Mississippi."

Then, mother held me oh, so tight.
She pulled me to her chest.
She started humming softly
While I tried to get some rest.

I didn't get to rest for long,
I heard muffled sounds outside.
It was the doctors huddled up
And our door was opened wide.

I heard one say, "I'll tell her.
She won't like the news I'll share.
This is hard to say to humans,
And no less, for hurting bears."

The doctor walked in timidly
Saying, "Ruth, you just can't go.
Our rules require you meet us there.
We wanted you to know."

Mom asked, "Why can't I ride with you?
I do not understand!"
One doctor said quite sheepishly,
"You won't fit in our van."

The doc was right, my mom was large.
She weighed 400 pounds.
She looked right good for a bear her age,
She could still turn heads around!

The doctor said, "I'm sorry Ma'am
Even if we squeezed you in,
Our tires would pop, our axles break!
We can call your next of kin."

"Just promise you'll take care of him.
He'll be scared and all alone.
Please do your best to make him well
And quickly bring him home."

The doctor said, "You know we will!
We'll make him good as new.
And when he's well I'll bring him home
And hand him back to you.

"He should be well in no time,
I predict three weeks or less.
Then you can hold and spoil him
And keep him at your chest."

Mom grabbed an old, red blanket then
That her mom gave to her.
She wrapped me up and swaddled me.
It warmed my brand-new fur.

She said, "This wrap will keep you safe.
Our love, for generations,
Is placed inside this special gift
To support tough situations.

"This blanket has a special power
It helps you understand
The history of the life of bears
Who once walked this special land.

"This blanket gives you wisdom
Beyond what you should know.
It will help you work with humans.
It will help you learn and grow.

"One day you will be able
To talk like humans do.
A child in need will launch this gift,
Then you can help him, too."

4

DAD'S "BEAR ESSENTIALS" CODE

Our bonding time was strong but brief,
My dad was unaware
That Mom had given birth to me...
Mom wanted him right there.

He was travelling near Atlanta.
He could be gone a while.
My mom looked at me helplessly
And she smiled a worried smile.

She told me, "Your dad loves you, son.
I'm sorry he's not here.
Please know our love is unified,
So half of him is near.

"The neighbors brought a jar of jam
For us to have tonight.
It's what your dad sells every day.
It will give you strength to fight.

"The jam has royal honey, and
Wild berries in the mix.
It's filled with magic from the bees.
There's not much this can't fix."

She said, "You're going to LOVE your dad.
He is strong and brave and smart.
That part of him is in you now
To support you and your heart.

"Before he left on his long trip
He wrote this CODE for you.
It is a guide, if you abide
That can help your heart stay true.

"Please, Eli, listen with your heart,
There's something you must hear.
We all live by this heart-based code.
I will state this very clear."

Dad's Bear Essentials Code:

Be who you are and know yourself.
Pretenders are not real.
Say what you mean and don't hold back.
Express the way you feel.

When you know yourself you can't be lost
And your life will take you far.
The key is being TRUE TO YOU
And remembering who you are.

Respect all life, it's here for you
And trust your heart to guide.
Know love surrounds you every day.
It never leaves your side.

Be still and quiet, you're not alone
And in your stillness hear
The whispers of a wise, sweet voice
Who cares for you, my dear.

Please, laugh and sing out every day.
Your joy expressed in sound
Can fill the hearts of those you love.
They're blessed when you're around.

Remember, every word and thought
Creates the world you'll see.
And say 'I Love You' every day....
And say it joyfully!

Dad's Bear Essentials Code:

Remember, you are special child
And have a precious gift,
And when you bring your gift to serve
The hearts you touch will lift.

There's no one else like you, my child,
You are stardust made from love.
Appreciate the life you have
And thank your stars above.

I promise you can change the world.
Allow your feelings to be felt.
And trust the wisdom of your heart
To let you be yourself.

One final message for your heart,
Its power will ring true:
I believe in you with all my heart
Now, YOU believe in YOU!

BEAR ESSENTIALS

Be who you are and know yourself.
Pretenders are not real.
Say what you mean and don't hold back.
Express the way you feel.

When you know yourself you can't be lost
And your life will take you far.
The key is being TRUE TO YOU
And remember who you are.

Respect all life, it's here for you
And trust your heart to guide,
know love surrounds you even...

As Mom finished her last sentence
A nurse peeked in the door
She said, "I know each minute's precious,
But you can only have five more."

That time went by in seconds flat
Then gowned folks rushed right in.
They said, "We have the van outside
To go take care of him."

Mom asked for just one minute more
She said, "We need some space."
She looked at me and cleared her throat.
As a tear ran down her face.

5

ELI'S SONG

Mom hugged me just before I left
And held me... oh, so long.
She sang to me a lullaby
And called it "Eli's Song."

Her words did echo in my heart,
The tune was soft and sweet.
Her every word filled me with hope
And urged my heart to beat.

Mom's Song for Me:

You'll never be alone my child
No matter where you are!
I'm always right here by your side,
Although it seems I'm far.

True love connects us one and all.
It gives our heart great wings.
We're meant to soar down here, sweet child.
You'll do such special things!

Now, in your heart I'll place this song
To guide you night and day,
And pray these words will keep you safe
To always light your way.

Your magic words are...Love Yourself.
This next word then is key.
In future days, if you feel pain
FORGIVENESS sets you free!

I share one final blessing, son,
My joy for you now sings.
If you feel lost, just touch your heart
And return to Copper Springs.

Just tune your "heart's ears" to the sound
Of rushing, gurgling streams
And see dragonflies swarm all around
As they cool us with their wings.

Mom's Song for Me:

Hear the sound of bear cubs playing
As their mothers all look on,
And feel the sacred presence of
The home where you belong.

True love connects us one and all.
It gives our heart great wings.
We're meant to soar down here, sweet child.
You'll do such special things!

Now, in your heart I'll place this song
To guide you night and day,
And pray these words will keep you safe
To always light your way.

As mother's song was finishing
A kind nurse came back in
She said, "It's time for us to go.
Let this journey now begin!

Her name was head nurse Julia
She put my mom at ease.
She said, "I have some news to share
I think you will be pleased.

"We'll get your baby home to you
Sometime in mid-December.
His surgery is two days from now,
I wrote it down, so you'll remember.

"I'll arrange for him to get back home.
They will bring him back to you.
Four weeks of care with time to heal
Will have him good as new."

Mom smiled and hugged nurse Julia
She then walked back to me
She said, "You're always in my heart
And forever there you'll be."

Mom promised she would send me notes
While I was far away.
She said, "You won't be gone too long.
Soon, you'll be home to stay."

She said, "600 miles is far,
But you won't be alone.
I'm sure your dad is on his way
And soon we'll all be home."

6

WELCOME TO HEROIC HEARTS HOSPITAL

Next thing I knew I was wrapped up
And anchored to a bed.
It had four wheels and handles, too,
And through the halls we sped.

They placed me in a long white car
With one red flashing light.
We sped away from my new world
And drove for half the night.

At dawn we reached the heart-care place
Where human babies go,
But it was far away from Mom...
I already missed her so!

They rolled me down a long white hall
Atop a metal cart.
The kids I passed had cords and tape
Connected to their hearts.

I was so tired and lonely.
I felt so out of place.
I was the only infant there
With fur all on my face!

7

THE KINDNESS OF A STRANGER

They took me to a treatment room
To check my troubled heart.
My fears had made it beat so fast
They wrote it on my chart.

One lady there, dressed all in white,
Pulled me up and to her chest.
She rocked me while she stood in place
And put my heart at rest.

This lady, known as Dora,
Called the doctors in to see
A little bear who needed care
So they could restore me.

The doctors said, "Don't worry, son!
Tomorrow we'll repair
Your little heart to make it strong
To beat like every bear!

"We'll have to make a little cut
To open up your chest.
We'll fix your heart and help it grow
Your heart will be the BEST!"

They asked the lady dressed in white
To take me down the hall
And place me in my special room
Until the next day's call.

Nurse Dora held me closely
As we walked the long, wide hall.
I felt the kids inside each room
(I was connected to them all!)

8

The New Kid on the Block

Nurse Dora took me to my room
She made me feel at home.
She introduced me to a boy
Who lay there all alone.

Nurse Dora said, "Hey, Billy Jones.
I have a friend for you.
He's from a town called Bear Ridge,
We're fixing his heart too!

"His name is Elijah Benjamin
He just arrived today.
He's going to be your roommate.
He lives one state away.

"His 'heart-hurt' is a lot like yours.
We hope he heals like you.
I know you're going to love him
We're glad to have him too."

Billy Jones was one odd creature.
Small dots danced 'cross his nose
His hair was red and square on top
He wore tight fitting clothes.

On Billy's neck he wore a brace.
He couldn't look at me
But I felt a bond between us both
It took no time to see.

This creature made me curious
I had to know much more
I grabbed my special blanket
And I tried hard not to roar.

I remembered what my mother said.
That one day I would speak,
And talk the way that humans do.
(And my first words would seem meek.)

I then released my first real words.
I had to find out more
About this kid named Billy Jones
Who convinced me not to roar.

I noticed Billy's squared off head.
It was such a funny shape!
I asked him, "Why's your head not round?"
He said, "Ain't my crew cut great?!"

He said, "It is the latest craze.
My friends have crew cuts too.
They all put beeswax right on top
Just a little dab will do!"

I asked, "What are those red dots
That cover up your nose?"
He said, "They call them freckles,
When the sun shines each one grows!"

I then asked, "Why's your neck and head
Inside that tall white trap?"
He said, "I had an accident
My neck was nearly snapped."

"What happened?" I asked Billy Jones
"You look like you're in pain."
Billy said, "Just never hula hoop
In a thunderstorm with rain!"

"What's a hula hoop?" I asked Billy.
"Did it put you in this place?"
Billy said, "It is a giant ring
Kids can twirl around their waist.

"But I like taking chances,
I thought, hey, what the heck?
So, I decided I'd ride my bike
With my hoop around my neck!

"I'm here because my heart got fixed
A couple months ago.
But the doctors made me come right back
This neck thing made it so."

I asked, "How did this circle thing
Make you come right back here?"
He said, "My silly bicycle
Got me stuck in second gear.

"It wasn't that the gear was bad
My problem was my hoop
I was twirling it around my neck
While my bike was turning loops!

"My last loop was a bad one
The rain locked up my brakes.
I swerved into my neighbor's tree
That was my first mistake.

"My second error in judgment
Was for riding in the rain
The lightning bolts struck all around
And sent my dog insane.

"That crazy pup ran into me
He swerved my bike off course
I veered into a dogwood tree
Those limbs had mighty force!

"I thought that I had cleared that tree
But one limb stopped my ride
It hooked my hoop and down I went
My neck was still inside.

"An ambulance came to get me
They brought me quickly here
They also brought my hula hoop
And my bike in second gear.

"I'm better now, believe me!
That limb became a log.
My Dad has cut that whole tree down
And worked hard to train my dog!"

I asked him then, "How old are you?"
He said, "I'm almost five!
Tomorrow is my birthday
I'm so happy I'm alive.

"I'm lucky Mama sent me here
Dora saw me at my worst.
She helped relieve my crazy fears
And put my feelings first."

Nurse Dora peeked into our room
And said, "Let's get some rest.
We have to pace ourselves a bit
You don't need added stress!"

Nurse Dora put my things away.
My blanket and Dad's jam
Some clothes, and toys my Grandma sent
And my boots to jump and stand.

Nurse Dora gave us each a hug
Before she left our room.
I watched her walk away from me
And hoped I'd see her soon.

9

WHY SPECIAL BEARS TALK

I was glad I had a roommate,
But Billy looked so tired.
He had a cut above his heart.
His chest was bruised and wired.

I asked him if he was OK
He said, "I cannot lie.
That surgery really wore me out."
"I'm so sorry," I replied.

I asked him, "Tell me where you're from?
How long have you been here?
Has your operation healed you yet?
And, did you have much fear?"

"Louisiana's my home state.
It had only been two weeks
Before my antics brought me back
When my poor neck got so tweaked!

"My surgery was two months ago
My heart's now not so weak
I started feeling better
When I learned a few techniques."

"What are techniques?" I then asked him.
He said, "A fancy word
That Dora calls her special help
To keep me undeterred."

I told him, "There you go again!
Undeterred, what does that mean?"
He said, "It means to not give up
Despite how hard things seem."

"Do five-year olds all use big words?
I'm used to speaking bear.
My English isn't all that good."
Then Billy turned to stare!

"I didn't know that bears could talk!"
Billy rubbed his eyes to see.
He turned his brace to see my face.
It was the first time he saw me!

"Of course, I talk!" I said to him.
"We must communicate.
I hear your thoughts before you speak.
Each word I then translate."

Billy asked me, "How'd you get like that?"
I told him, "Evolution!
Not just by me, but all life's bears
In our five-million-year solution."

"Were bears here before us humans?
How long have we been here?"
I said, "Two-Hundred Thousand years.
But that number's not too clear.

"Bears have adapted many times
To inhabit Earth with man.
We've come to know your thoughts and ways
Though you're hard to understand.

"See, humans hurt the things they need.
Like water, soil and air.
They harm the balance of all life.
We think most just don't care.

"We've learned to talk to make more friends
And help folks understand.
We're on this planet all as one
We are all in nature's plan.

"Our mothers teach us from day one
To respect life... big and small.
The Earth is like one great big home.
She is sacred to us all!"

Then Billy uttered quietly.
"How special you must be!
My mother says I'm special, too.
We might change history!"

I laughed and said, "But not tonight!
I need to get some rest.
I have a big day coming up,
I need me at my best!"

Then Billy turned off all the lights.
So we could get some sleep,
While the box connected to his chest
Kept pinging: BEEP, BEEP, BEEP!

10

MOTHER'S NOTE

I tried real hard to go to sleep,
But the noise kept me awake.
My mind and heart just could not rest.
My fears were hard to take.

My room was big and had machines
Beside my bed with rails.
There was a box with flashing lights
That shared my heart's details.

The biggest noise was Billy!
His snoring pierced the air.
It was a wheezing, sneezing sound
That sent chills through my hair!

Beside me was a button,
And when I pushed it down,
A nurse would run into my room.
Sometimes she had a frown.

I buzzed three times for Dora
I prayed that she was there.
I came to trust her most of all.
She always brought great care.

Ten minutes later Dora came.
She peeked inside the room.
She didn't want to wake up Billy
So, she whisked in like a broom.

She asked, "What is the matter child?
Why are you buzzing so?"
I said, "The noise is loud in here
Is there somewhere else to go?"

She said, "I've got a gift for you
It should put your mind at ease.
It just arrived this evening
I know that you'll be pleased."

It was a message from my mom.
There also was a card.
Nurse Dora read them both to me
Then said, "I know it's hard.

"The other kids have moms and dads
Who visit them each day.
But your mommy cannot get here.
'Cause she lives so far away.

"Six-hundred miles is quite a ways
For a bear who has no car.
She said that she had tried to walk
But didn't get too far."

Mom's note said, "Dad just got the news.
He read our wire today.
He knows you're having surgery, so
He's hitchhiking back our way."

She said, "Your dad's a salesman
He travels near and far.
He sells a brand of honey
And makes 50 cents a jar!

"He's so sorry that he wasn't here
He was very far away,
You came sooner than expected
You just made your own birthday!

"My son, you live in Bear Ridge,
A small town in Tennessee,
Tucked in the northeast corner
With amazing sites to see.

"Your community is called Copper Springs
For the stream that runs through town.
It flows off Turtle Lakes with joy
And it makes a gurgling sound."

Dora said, "It'll take some time for family
To come and be with you.
So, I will serve as best I can
To make it up to you."

Then from the card nurse Dora found
Another great surprise.
It was a photo of my mom.
Some tears came to my eyes.

Dora took the photo of my mom
And placed it to my chest.
I felt a great deal more at peace.
I tried to get some rest.

It was good to see my mother's face
Even though it was a picture.
It added hope that I'd be fine
It brightened up my "ticker."

Mom's loving face made me feel safe,
The noises seemed to scatter.
My fears then left me all at once
My mind heard no more chatter.

Nurse Dora made the whole room still.
She made the noises drown.
She leaned down close to kiss my head.
I was glad she was around.

She was the kindest stranger
That I had ever met.
I knew she would become a friend
I never would forget!

"Now get some rest, my little bear.
I'll wake you up at five.
You have a busy day ahead.
We are here to help you thrive."

I pled then, "Please, help Billy too!
He is making awful sounds.
Can you pinch those freckles on his nose?
To make his noises drown!"

She smiled and said, "I'm sorry child
I can't do that to him.
Here, try these plastic earplugs
To make those noises dim."

I plugged those gadgets in my ears
Then felt a peaceful quiet.
I said goodnight to Dora
Having won the beep/snore riot!

II

My Inner Hero

I slept in peace for hours.
I then awoke at three.
I dreamed of mother's blanket
All wrapped up to protect me.

I then heard Mom's voice singing
Sending love from Copper Springs,
Her lullaby was still in me
I felt the comfort her tune brings.

I knew then I would be all right,
I knew I would survive.
I felt my heart beat YES to me.
I felt it smile inside.

I looked around my heart-care room.
I saw shadows on my wall.
I had not noticed until then
These forms both large and small.

A crack beneath my sturdy door
Let light creep in my room
It cast a brilliance on the wall.
It lifted any gloom.

My special room was colorful.
The walls were filled with art
Of super heroes now assigned
To protect my ailing heart.

One superhero had a cape,
His face was brave and strong.
I felt his courage whispering,
"You'll be well before too long."

His cape looked like the blanket
That Mom had given me.
I knew it had the power
To set my young fears free!

I took my special blanket then,
And placed it 'round my neck.
I thought it made me look real cool.
(My mirror let me check.)

As I looked at my reflection
I felt a sense of pride.
My parent's words came back to me
And touched me deep inside.

I heard the words, "Be who you are!"
"Respect all life," "Be kind."
And, "Trust your heart to guide you, son,"
"Seek peace in heart and mind."

"Be still, be quiet and listen.
All answers, you must know.
Are waiting for you in your heart.
Your wisdom wants to show."

And then I heard the word "Believe"
I looked up on my shelf.
To see a photo of my mom
With her reminder, *LOVE YOURSELF!*

Then, magically I saw these words
Take on a thread-like shape,
They wove themselves into the fabric
Of my hero's cape!

These woven words of wisdom
Were now a part of me,
Great wisdom from my ancestors
I could access easily.

I felt them all gaze down at me.
I was warmed by lasting love.
I felt their special guiding hands
Now hold me from above.

That night I wrapped myself up tight
Inside my hero's cape
And heard Mom's words inside my heart
Bound, never to escape.

Then, I thought about my missing Dad.
I knew I'd meet him soon.
I'd need his love to help me heal
To quickly leave this room!

I wondered what he looked like.
Was he large or was he thin?
Why did he go so far away?
And did I look like him?

Then I prayed my mom and dad would come
And both stand next to me,
And that we all would join as one
As a loving family.

Though far away, my parents
Were connected to me now.
I felt them both watch over me
I'd see them soon somehow!

This night as I lay down to sleep,
I felt LOVE circle me.
It filled my heart with peace and trust
So, my mind could now be free.

My sleep came softly in the night.
I dreamed that I was home,
Surrounded by my mom and dad,
No longer all alone.

12

Good Morning

The next day came so early.
Before the sun could shine,
A lady dressed in red pinstripes
Said, "Hey Eli, it is time!"

She asked me, "Did you sleep OK?"
I said, "Finally, I slept fine!"
I asked her, "Are the doctors set
To fix this heart of mine?"

She assured me they were well-prepared
To make me good as new.
She told me then to do the things
I thought I'd need to do.

I washed my face and brushed my teeth
Then put my cape in place.
I heard a voice outside my door,
Then saw Ms. Dora's face.

She said, "Hello my special friend!
I'm here to care for you
And keep your mommy up to date
On everything we do!"

Billy Jones woke up and said out loud,
"And what am I, chopped liver?
I thought I was your favorite friend
And you, my great caregiver."

Dora said, "Good Morning, Billy!
I have no favorites here.
You all are special kids to me.
You each bring me great cheer.

"I remember just two months ago
The day I came to you
To wake you up to take you in
To get your heart fixed, too.

"You were so brave that special day,
And now it's Eli's turn.
Let's put our love for his best care.
Today, he's our concern."

Billy said, "Good Morning, Eli,
I'm sorry I'm so grumpy.
This neck brace makes me restless
And my mattress is too lumpy!

"I didn't sleep a wink last night.
I'll sleep more tonight I'm hopin'."
I said, "Your winks worked long enough,
'Cause you don't snore with your eyes open!"

Nurse Dora said, "Go back to sleep,
But wish your friend the best.
He'll need your friendship late today,
You'll both need added rest."

Billy Jones then closed his restless eyes,
His words bounced off the wall
"Good luck, Eli, you will be fine,
We are in this one and all."

Nurse Dora added, "Yes we are.
Eli, know while you stay,
I'll give to you my very best
To help you heal each day.

"I'm glad you finally fell asleep!
You needed all your rest.
To have your heart prepare to mend
And beat stronger in your chest!

"You are my little hero here!
You're as special as can be.
I feel the powers of your cape
That magic we can't see."

She said, "Heroes make good choices.
They take care of themselves.
They don't ride bikes with hula hoops,
Or smash neighbor's cute yard elves!"

Billy raised his head a moment
He asked, "Who told you that?
I glued it back together.
I hate when Mom chit-chats!"

Nurse Dora chided Billy,
"Foolish choices hurt more than you.
Your new heart's not invincible.
Your mom wants what's best for you.

"Riding in the rain with hula hoops
Is more than your heart needs.
You have to give it time to heal
And avoid big cuts that bleed!

"Don't take your heart for granted.
It's important you stay well.
Watch what you eat and what you say,
You are the temple where it dwells."

Nurse Dora said, "Go back to sleep.
Eli and I need time."
She then leaned closer into me
And said, "You'll be just fine."

13

MY NEW HEROIC HEART

Dora touched my chest and said, "THIS heart
That beats inside of you.
Will be strong and quite invincible,
There'll be nothing you can't do!"

She said, "Love is a power
That lives inside each heart.
It's up to us to help it grow,
So we can do our part."

She said her heart was broken once,
So many years ago.
But, she had learned to mend it back,
She said LOVE made it so.

Dora asked me, "Are you ready now,
To conquer this big day?
In hours you'll be good as new.
I'll be with you all the way!"

I said, "Yes, Ma'am, I'm ready!
Will they use scissors and some tape?
Please, tell them I'm an only child
And be sure I have my cape!"

She smiled and said, "You'll be just fine.
I'll have your cape with me.
The doctors do this all the time.
They're as trained as they can be!"

I asked, "But do they work on bears?"
I just see boys and girls.
They have no fur or whiskers and
We live in different worlds!"

Billy stirred from playing possum
He said, "A heart is just a heart!
You'll only have to lay there, and
Let the doctors do their part."

He said, "There's nothing to this.
They put you fast asleep.
When you wake up, you'll be brand new,
And your heart will have great beeps!"

Nurse Dora said, "Don't think too much.
They know just what to do.
They'll fix your heart just like the rest
And make you good as new!"

She told me that this one event
Would forever be the day
Where I faced my fears with courage
So, my heart could lead the way.

She said, "Your new heroic heart
Will guide you past all fear
And soon the power of your heart
Will serve you well, my dear."

I got into my wheelchair then.
Nurse Dora guided me.
I pulled more tightly on my cape
And felt my family.

As we rolled along nurse Dora said,
"Eli, you need to know,
There's a Great Bear Spirit in the sky,
Who sees all and loves you so!"

She said, "Great Bear is with you now,
It's holding your mom too.
The Great Bear loves you night and day
And, it's here to see you through.

I asked Dora if she knew Great Bear
She said, "Love takes many forms.
For bears it is more furry,
But for all, love is the norm."

"It is funny how we name things
And we never understand,
Some mysteries just can't be named
And that's a lesson in LOVE's plan.

Dora said, "Just know LOVE'S here for you.
It can go by any name,
Please know that you're a part of it
And it loves us all the same.

I then felt Great Bear holding me.
It wrapped me in its arms.
It whispered, "CHILD, I LOVE YOU,
And your heart will not be harmed."

Dora rolled me to a big bright room.
I felt my eyes grow tired...
I woke up in a different place.
My chest was shaved and wired!

14

MY ZIPPERED HEART

I heard someone say, "Recovery Room."
Everything was slow and blurred.
The noises all were muffled sounds.
My sign said, "Don't Disturb."

When I woke up I felt real strange,
I felt lost and confused.
I heard someone say, "He's waking up!"
My chest was sore and bruised.

My eyes felt glued and lift-less.
I was groggy and had pain.
My chest was swollen from my cuts.
My energy had waned.

I had a heart-shape on my chest
With stitches in the center.
I saw a door let more light in
Then, I heard my doctor enter.

My stitches seemed to be okay.
The doc said, "You did great!
You'll need more time in here to heal,
And man, I dig your cape!"

Nurse Dora came to check on me.
She brought with her a mirror.
She said, "It's time for you to see
Your heart a little clearer."

I saw the stitches on my heart.
My chest fur shaved away.
My naked skin was heart-shaped now
(But it wouldn't stay that way!)

Nurse Dora saw I wore my cape
And said I seemed more "chipper."
I smiled and touched each careful stitch
That looked just like a zipper!

Nurse Dora said, "Each beating heart
Has zippers we can't see.
Some zip them up and live in pain,
That zipping down relieves.

"Your heart's like new," nurse Dora said.
"And can better serve you now.
We will work together, you and I.
We'll release you soon somehow."

I then thought about my mother
And prayed that she would know
That I could now let more love in
And allow my joy to grow!

I remembered mother's song to me
And how she held me tight.
The words still echoed in my heart
To give me great delight:

"You'll never be alone my child
No matter where you are!
I'm always here right by your side,
Although it seems I'm far.

True love connects us one and all.
It gives our heart great wings.
We're meant to soar down here, sweet child.
You'll do such special things!"

Two-hours later I was wheeled right back
Into my room with Billy.
My recovery had gone just as planned
Except my feet were chilly!

15

BILLY'S SPECIAL GIFT

That night I slept just like a champ.
Recovery work was hard!
I dreamed my chest was better now
But I checked, it was still scarred.

The "sleeping potion" had worn off
But things were still real hazy.
As my eyes peeked out beneath my lids
I thought that I'd gone crazy.

I saw a blotch of red and flesh.
The blurry thing had dots.
Its head was square and stuck straight up.
Its eyes were small blue spots.

The blotched thing moved and said aloud,
"Hey nurse, can he see clearly?
I've been waiting for him by his bed.
It's been three hours, nearly!"

He said, "Hey Bud! It's Billy Jones.
Dora said I could sit here."
He said, "The worst part's over now."
Then he grinned from ear to ear.

He said, "You talk when you're asleep!
You mumbled something strange.
You said you had to run away.
The plan had been arranged."

I said, "I know of no such plan.
It's not my time to leave.
I'm just here to get healthy.
I've got nothing up my sleeve!"

Billy said, "I know the pain you feel.
I had to feel it too.
My neck surgery was two weeks ago,
So, I'm here to pull for you."

He said, "Each day is different.
Sometimes you feel alone.
That's why I'm sitting by your side.
It's a hard fight on your own."

He then gave me a present
Saying, "She helped me through my pain.
My sister gave this as a gift
Now I'm doing just the same."

It was a sweet stuffed rabbit,
Her name, 'Ms. Flops-A-Lot.'
She was soft and very cuddly.
Her white belly, one big spot.

Billy said, "You need her more than me.
Please keep her by your side.
She listens to each word you say.
She was my loving guide.

"You can tell her secrets from your heart
She's a trusted friend, you'll see.
She's a loving, soft companion
Who can see the best in me."

Billy said, "One day there'll come a time
When someone needs more love.
Then you can pass her on to them
In a gift of pure, true love."

I then thanked Billy for his gift.
I now had one more friend.
Ms. Flopsy would be there for me
And become my true godsend.

As Billy crawled back in his bed
He chuckled with great glee.
I asked, "What made you laugh so loud?"
He said, "You snore much worse than me!"

16

MY SUPERHERO POWER

Dora said, "It's time to know your heart,
I am blessed to be your guide.
I'll help you to expand your heart
While leaving it inside.

She asked me, "Are you ready, child?
Today is your big day!
I'm going to share my heart with you
To help love guide your way."

She told me that my weakness
Was my strength right from the start.
That over time, with love, I'd build
My own HEROIC HEART.

She said, "I want to let you know
There's a world we cannot see.
It loves us deeply and just wants
To guide both you and me.

"This unseen force protects us.
It helps us when we're lost.
It brings true value to this world.
It does this free of cost.

"This loving force will work with you
But you must learn to ask
The questions of your patient heart
To prepare you for each task.

"It comes to you through feelings
To help you see and hear
The beauty that surrounds you, child,
And helps you conquer fear.

"These gifts I now will share with you
To support you with life's tasks.
To gain this wisdom you must learn
To LISTEN, FEEL and ASK!

"And when you master these three things
Each moment of each hour,
Your heroic heart down here on Earth
Becomes your superpower!

"The super power of listening
Makes your ears attuned to life
You hear the words and feel their truth
And know each word feels right.

"The super power of feeling
Helps you feel and trust the truth.
Your heart will always know what's right
Your heart's a super sleuth!

"The super power of asking,
Allows your heart to bring
Such precious treasures to your life-
Hearts uncover everything!

"Once you feel and trust the truth you seek
Then your 'asking' will be stronger.
The power of connecting both
Makes life's joy last so much longer.

"But, asking can't be wanting.
It's surrendering to grace.
Invite the life your heart desires
Then the magic falls in place.

"There's so much more your heart will share
But first believe in YOU.
Your trust and grace can then join hands
To make your dreams come true."

I pulled Ms. Flopsy to my chest
And hugged her for a while
I think she listened to my heart
Because I saw her smile.

17

LOVE CONQUERS FEAR

My next day's lesson was in bed.
Dora came into my room.
She invited Billy to listen in.
He could help her, I assumed.

First, Dora showed a chart to me.
It was a great big heart.
She said each heart holds wisdom
That our trust could then impart.

She said that many lessons here
Teach us to be aware
Of ways to let us know our hearts
And help us build self-care.

Then Dora gave me some advice,
"A strong heart's filled with joy!"
She said, "Our joy subdues our fears.
And fear makes us destroy.

"It's fear that wants to shut love out
So, courageous you must be,
We're heroes all in waiting here.
Please set your hero free!"

She said the heart loves simple things
That it can do each day,
Like making friends and being kind,
To laugh and sing and play.

"We're meant to make a joyful noise.
Our songs help spirits rise,
And laughing can make others smile.
Look for hearts in people's eyes."

Billy said, "I think that's why I snore!
It's a joyful noise to me.
I just can't hear it while I sleep
'Cause I'm just to tired, you see!"

"Well, not quite," nurse Dora said aloud.
"I meant a better sound.
But I'm certain that you make hearts smile
Whenever you're around!"

She also said, "The heart is served
By being kind to all.
The heart will grow when we are nice
To creatures large and small."

As I listened to each word she said
My chest began to swell.
My heart knew it could grow and heal
Each stitch could soon be well.

As daylight yawned and evening grew
Nurse Dora said good night.
Her words left me determined now
To love with all my might!

18

DID YOU HEAR THAT?

The next day nudged me from my sleep.
My pain left in my dreams.
My rugged stitches, all smoothed out,
They felt like precious seams.

The remaining scars were healing fast.
My heart was stronger too!
The seams around my grateful heart
Looked like a red tattoo.

My heart-shaped outline had a glow.
Nurse Dora saw it shine.
She told me love can heal all wounds.
It happens all the time!

Then Dora said, "Today's your day!
Your heart is ready now.
When your heart glows, the magic starts,
And old thoughts shift somehow.

"Let's start with listening, precious child.
You hear more than you know.
Your mind hears whispers from your heart
Which helps you trust and grow.

"First, let's both try something easy.
Close your eyes, shut down the noise,
Tune into something that you love,
Perhaps your mom or toys.

"We will call this practice, 'wakeful sleep'
You feel asleep, but you're awake.
Your awareness is much more in tune
To hear each breath you take.

"Let's focus on the roses now
That your mother sent to you.
Put your focus on that budding rose...
See if it can speak, too!"

I then got really quiet,
Closed my eyes and listened clear.
I tuned in to each breath I took
And I asked my heart to hear.

I put my ears on 'super hear'
That bud faintly made a sound
It whispered from across the room,
"I am glad that you're around!"

The rosebud said, "I sit for days
And no one hears my song.
I sing it every minute here
Yet, no one sings along."

I listened to her blooming song.
It was peaceful and serene.
I watched each note float joyously.
They were misty waves of green.

The rose then told me secrets.
She said, "Flowers all can heal!
We send out waves called frequencies.
Our sweet power's strong and real.

"That's why humans send out flowers.
Our vibration's fragrant smell
Can lift the spirits of the sick
And help make people well."

I thanked the bud for her sweet song
And asked her for her name.
She said, "I'm Dew Drop Wendy.
I love wind and sun and rain."

I then heard Ms. Flopsy say,
"I hear you sing each day!
I hum a little while you sing
Your songs take my breath away!"

I said, "I didn't know you talked!
Do I need to clean my ears?"
She said, "We all talk every day
To sweet souls prepared to hear."

I asked, "Does Billy know you talk?"
She said, "I tried, he couldn't hear.
You're different Eli Benjamin,
My heart's whispers fill your ear."

I asked, "Can Dora hear you now?"
She said, "My voice is just for you.
It will be here when you need me
I will help you see what's true."

Flopsy winked and then went silent,
As nurse Dora called my name.
She asked me, "Did your heart hear well?"
I said, "I can't explain!

"I heard a rose bud blooming.
Ms. Flopsy talked to me.
I felt tuned in to all of life.
It was a listening fantasy!"

Nurse Dora smiled quite knowingly.
She hugged me with delight.
She tucked Ms. Flopsy in my bed
And told us both good night.

19

HOW DOES IT FEEL?

The next day's lesson, number two,
Was all about my feelings.
Dora said, "Your feelings never lie,
Their truth is most revealing."

She said, "Dear Eli, you must know
Your heart feels everything!
Your feelings are your special guide
That give your wisdom wings.

"One thing I do is touch my chest
And breathe in deep three times.
When I am through I ask my heart
A question from my mind.

"I listen then real quietly.
My heart can speak to me.
I feel the answer that it gives
And know that I agree!"

Billy Jones then butted in and said,
"Oh yeah! I do that now.
Dora showed me how to do it,
And it always works somehow.

"For example, only days ago
I had to make a choice.
I put my hand right on my chest
And listened for its voice.

"My choice was keep Ms. Flopsy
Or, to give her to a friend.
As you can see, my choice was wise
And it had a joyful end."

Nurse Dora said, "I'm proud of you.
Ms. Flopsy's brand new start
With Eli has helped all of you.
I love gifts from the heart."

Nurse Dora then turned back to me
She said, "Please, trust your feelings!
Just learn to ask, then know to trust
This practice is revealing."

When Dora left, I touched my heart
And asked, "Where is my mom?"
I saw her face and felt her warmth,
And knew where I belonged.

I felt the words she sang to me
So many weeks ago,
My eyes were filled with tears of joy,
I wanted her to know.

In that moment I felt mother's love.
I experienced her heart.
And knew right then, no matter what,
We'd never be apart.

I held my blanket close to me,
It hugged me in return.
My blanket knew I'd be okay.
My blanket helped me learn.

I then thanked all my ancestors
For their gift Mom gave to me.
Together, wrapped in loving thoughts,
My new heart now could see!

20

ASK AWAY!

The next day Dora smiled and said,
"We've now reached lesson three.
We'll learn the power of asking
From a heart that's filled with glee.

"See, giving and receiving
Are a loop in love's sweet game.
They play together all the time.
They are nearly just the same.

"When we are in a place of joy
And filled with gratitude,
Great Spirit Bear smiles down on us
And our gifts can be accrued.

"When we love others as ourselves
Abundance opens up.
Our giving turns the faucet on
And lets us fill our cup.

"This flow allows our heart's desires
To activate a need.
Great Spirit Bear knows every wish
And helps us to succeed.

"Ask from a place of loving.
Place desires within your heart.
Then give to others joyfully
And watch the magic start."

Nurse Dora said, "Our heart's desires
Have been placed in us to see
The dreams we will hold in our hand
When we ask, then hear, we'll see.

"Let's start with understanding.
The universe needs you
To help create things from your heart
That only you can do.

"We each have very special gifts
And talents here to give.
They're meant to make life better.
They bring joy to how we live.

"Your gift will be your loving heart.
Your desires can all be filled.
When you ask and trust each outcome
Your heart holds breathless thrills.

"Great Spirit Bear wants to help us out.
But we must trust and ask.
Our words are always heard and felt.
Great Bear just loves this task.

"Great Bear loves deep connection;
It finds so many ways.
It whispers words. It brings new friends.
It loves us every day.

"I love when Great Bear uses signs
To speak to me sometimes.
It's not the kind on streets or roads.
They are so much less defined.

"A sign may be a song you hear
When you are feeling low.
That song may offer words to you
Straight from your radio.

"The words and signs are meant for you.
They speak right to your heart.
It feels like magic when it comes.
It gives you a fresh start.

"One thing I do to see what's true,
I ask to see a sign.
It comes in ways I don't expect
But it always comes in time.

"The key to signs is BE ALERT!
They're packaged beautifully.
They're not as obvious as you'd hope.
So you must be prepared to see.

"These all are ways to guide your path.
Please, use them anytime.
It just takes practice every day
To hush your busy mind."

Nurse Dora gave me confidence.
With fear I now could cope.
She told me she believed in me.
She offered love and hope.

I learned hope is a precious thing.
It helps remove frustration.
It sets us on a path to grow
With loving expectation.

Belief is knowing something
You can't see but trust is there.
I put trust in the Great Bear now
To help my heart repair.

And as the day pulled down its shade
I asked to get a sign
To let me know I'd make it through
This "trust-your-heart-now" time.

I looked out of my window then
To ask The Great Bear this,
"Can you please let me know for sure
That you hear me and exist?"

Flopsy perked up then and said to me
"Every thought and word is heard.
Be patient, time can test you, friend,
Try being graceful like a bird."

Then I saw two sparrows fly outside,
A small one flew behind,
And I knew then Mom, Dad and I
Together would be fine.

21

CONNECTING DEEPER

The next day I told Dora.
About the birds and sign I saw.
I said, "It just seemed magical.
It filled my heart with awe."

She told me, "Great Bear wants to give
Your heart's desire with joy.
It just takes trust and strong belief
To receive these gifts, dear boy.

"One thing I do is get real quiet
And ask Great Bear these things.
I listen for love's answers
And I write the words LOVE brings.

"I ask it simple questions like...
'Why do you love me so?'
I listen then, with all my heart,
And write what I now know.

"I keep a journal every day
Of every conversation.
It helps me practice listening
And releases my frustration."

When Dora left I looked within
And asked The Great Bear this,
"Why did you give me this weak heart?
And why do I exist?"

I listened loud, I listened long.
I heard a thought so true.
YOU'RE HERE TO SHOW THE FOLKS DOWN THERE
THERE'S NOTHING THEY CAN'T DO!

YOUR HEART CAN OPEN EVERY DOOR.
YOUR LOVE INVITES LIFE IN.
YOU HAD TO UNDERSTAND YOUR HEART
TO KNOW THAT I'M YOUR FRIEND!"

I asked The Great Bear, "Are we friends?
I've never seen your face.
You're more like words that talk to me.
Are you from outer space?"

I AM THE FRIEND THAT'S ALWAYS HERE,
THE KIND WHO KNOWS YOUR HEART.
I KNEW YOU LONG BEFORE YOU CAME
I'VE KNOWN YOU FROM LIFE'S START.

I AM THE ONE WHO LISTENS,
I AM THE ONE WHO SHARES.
I AM THE ONE WHO LOVES YOU SO,
I AM THE ONE WHO CARES.

I AM THE VOICE OF DORA,
I AM THE HEART OF MOM,
I AM THE FATHER YOU DON'T KNOW,
I AM YOUR PEACE AND CALM.

I LOVE TO MEET YOUR TRUEST NEEDS,
JUST KNOW I'M ALWAYS HERE.
I'M WITH YOU EVERY BREATH YOU TAKE.
I LOVE YOU, ELI DEAR.

22

A Blizzard is Coming!

As days passed by I grew and grew.
I doubled in my size.
My fur got dark, my shaved chest healed,
I felt more brave and wise.

The fur around my chest came back
My heart got stronger, too.
I became connected to my heart.
It told me what to do.

One day my heart said, "Now it's time!
Please be prepared to leave.
Your mom and dad both need you now.
Please listen and believe!"

I ran to Dora then to ask,
"How soon can I go home?"
She said, "I'll call your doctor now.
I'll get him on the phone."

She said, "I know you're better now,
But I can't let you go.
I need the doctors to approve,
Then they can tell us so."

She tried and tried to reach my doc.
Her calls would not go through.
She said the phone would not connect.
Just why, she had no clue!

Then all at once it made more sense
A news flash on TV,
Declared, "A winter storm is near
It might make history!

"A winter blizzard's on its way!"
The weatherman sounded doomed.
"The phone lines here are all jammed up.
Be calm and please stay tuned."

Then Dora's face looked worried.
"This news is really bad!
If this snow hits, it may take months
To see your mom and dad!"

23

WHAT IS HIBERNATION?

I told nurse Dora, "I have no fear
Of the coming blizzard's snow!"
She said, "The problem's not the storm.
There's more you need to know!"

She said, "Most bears take real long naps
When winter weather nears.
They sleep until warm weather comes
Or, until the snow all clears.

"I know this news is hard to hear.
It may cause you frustration,
But winter season lets bears know
It's time for *hibernation!*"

She said that hibernation was
A part of nature's plan
To help the bears save energy
When snow deeply hits the land.

I then asked Dora, "Will I sleep
A long time like each bear?
When will this happen? Where's the snow?
How should I get prepared?"

She told me I had little time
For it was getting late.
She'd have me ready to go home
Before I'd hibernate.

I said, "I'll pray that Mom and Dad
Are now both safe at home
And that, I too, will join them there,
No longer on my own!"

I grabbed Ms. Flopsy and asked her this
"Are you brave enough to leave?"
She looked at me through plastic eyes
Saying, "I am if you believe."

I knew then that my time was short.
There could be no delay.
No matter what the doctors said
I knew I could not stay.

I'd plan my trip tomorrow.
But how could I escape?
I couldn't walk straight out the door
Or fly off with my cape!

I'd sleep on it that evening
Perhaps my dreams could show
A way for me to leave this place
Before the winter snow!

24

THE MYSTERIOUS THIEF

I tried to sleep with one eye closed,
The other half awake.
To doze off now and sleep for months
Would be a BIG mistake!

Then, late that night at ten p.m.,
I heard a rustling sound.
I peeked out from my hero's cape,
Glanced up.... then, all around.

Flopsy said to me, "Let's check it out!"
So, we both snuck out of bed.
I tiptoed quietly toward the sound
That filled my heart with dread!

The kitchen seemed to be the place
Where all this noise arose.
I slowly pushed the door ajar
Just using my big nose.

My bear's nose told me there was food.
It was a kitchen raid!
I tried to see the hungry thief
(Although I was afraid.)

As I pushed through the kitchen door
I caught the thief off guard.
He screamed aloud, raced up the wall
And hit the ceiling hard!

He pushed through one big ceiling tile
To make his quick escape,
While I found empty sandwich bags
And three jams he couldn't take.

The label said: "Original
Grandpaw Droopy Drawers -
Honey-Beary Jam's for You,
Now in your favorite stores."

It was a name I'd heard before
I could not remember where,
I thought it strange for jars of jam
To feature one old bear!

I put two jars back in the fridge,
The other stayed with me.
I'd have it as my midnight snack
To give me energy!

Then Flopsy spoke as I stood there
She said, "I love that jam!
I had it once with Billy Jones
On crackers he called graham.

"Those mid-day treats were wonderful.
His mother made great snacks.
Those crackers bring back memories.
He always ate three stacks!"

Then up above I heard the noise
That brought us to this room
Ms. Flopsy and I both looked up
To see a shadow loom.

We saw the creature peeking down.
With two little beady eyes.
I spoiled his snack, but he'd be back.
He was 'bout half my size.

I picked up all the mess he made,
Then slipped back to my room.
I knew that we would meet again.
I hoped it would be soon!

Flopsy smiled, "You're such a clean freak!
You never leave a mess.
Billy never was like this at all.
I like that you're obsessed!

"I say that cleanliness is good.
It shows such great respect
For you and others in your space
Instead of thinking, 'what the heck'?"

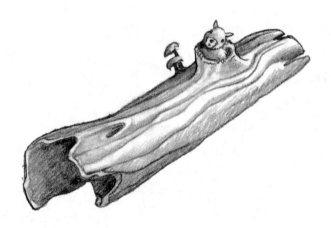

25

THE TALKING BOX

My wish to see the creature soon
Came quickly that same night
When I heard the sound of screaming pleas.
His cries were filled with fright!

I ran back to the kitchen ...but
The creature wasn't there.
His screams came from another room.
With a sign that said, "BEWARE!"

I peeked in through the keyhole.
I saw a box inside.
Whatever was within that box
Just cried and cried and cried!

The door had two protective locks.
The first was on the knob,
The second was a padlock chain
(This room was hard to rob.)

The box was filled with little holes.
It sat there on the ground.
Then all at once a nose popped out,
It made a sniffling sound.

The heavy box then spoke to me,
"Is that a bear I smell?
Please, help me out. I must escape!
Please, help me... I won't tell!"

"Why are you in that box?" I asked,
"Are you the thief I saw?"
The creature told me, "Yes I am!
I smelled some fresh coleslaw!"

He said, "I came to steal more food
But a man behind the door
Threw this box up on top of me
And said, 'You'll eat no more.'

"Dear bear, you just can't leave me here.
I am scared of small, tight places!
I am used to getting out of jams
And never leaving traces!"

I felt confused and had to choose.
Should I let him out of that box?
Was I doing something very wrong?
And could I break those locks?

I closed my eyes and touched my heart
I asked, "What should I do?"
The voice came quickly just for me
I felt its love come through.

In that moment I felt humbled,
I heard the voice of right and wrong.
I had not heard this voice before
To whom did it belong?

The voice said, "Hello, Eli.
I AM your thoughts of choice.
You are the one decider,
Your moral code's true voice.

"I AM the voice inside of you
That asked, 'Should I help out?
Or should I let this creature be?'
Your decision can't leave doubt."

The answer soon surprised me.
I heard, "You can't know everything.
What would you want if you were him?
There's a consequence life brings."

I thought about me trapped inside
A box with little holes,
With no way out and locked inside,
I had reversed our roles.

My heart said, "You would want let out.
It is hard to see folks suffer.
If you can let this creature go
You'll create a karmic buffer."

I asked what is a karmic buffer?
I heard, "A kindness that's recorded.
Great Bear keeps up with all of us,
And good deeds get rewarded.

"The same is true when we don't do
The right things in each moment.
We often get what we put out
The Great Bear makes us own it!"

I decided then that I would help
This poor creature I'd let go.
I was glad to know that goodness pays
To reap just what I'd sow.

This was my first true moral choice,
I would help this creature out.
My heart agreed as Flopsy smiled
This choice left me no doubt.

26

LAUGHING AT DANGER

I asked the creature for his name.
He said, "I'm Rascal Roy!
I love to steal food from the fridge
And stuff my face with joy!"

I felt bad for that Rascal guy.
Then Roy called out to me,
"Who trapped me here, and who are you?
Please, help me to get free!"

I told him, "I am Eli Bear.
We're in a heart-care place.
My heart was weak but soon I'll leave.
I have no time to waste!

"My mother had to send me here
To heal this heart of mine.
So, I was forced two weeks ago
To leave her far behind."

I then heard Rascal start to laugh
He said, "That name's divine!
From now on I will think of you as,
ELI BEAR BEHIND!"

I smiled at Rascal's cleverness.
That name made me laugh, too!
I knew that he would be my friend
And what I had to do!

I'd find a way to get him out.
A plan is what I'd need.
I had to make this rescue quick.
To get poor Rascal freed!

He said, "You know I'll help you.
I know my way around.
I've been sneaking here for two long years
And until now was not found.

"I promise if you let me out,
I will help you on your trip.
I'd love to travel as your pal
And stay right by your hip.

"I knew when I first met you
That you were kind and smart.
We both can help each other,
Tonight will be our start!"

27

OUR SNEAKY PLAN

He said, "Sneak back into your room
And quickly pack your clothes.
Then, grab your biggest pillowcase
Our escape must be like pros!

"Don't come back down the hallway.
We'll be doomed around midnight.
That's when the guards start their patrol.
Security's very tight!

"We'll keep our movements stealthy.
We'll have to work up high.
The best path is the ceiling,
So we'll pass those guards right by!

"When you get your goodies in your bag
Jump three times on your bed.
Punch out the ceiling tiles above.
That's how my friends have fled.

"There's a map my friends created,
It details every room.
From the ceiling we'll see all below
To spot danger that might loom.

"The map's above the kitchen
Your nose will take you there.
You'll have to be a sneaky thief.
Are you a sneaky bear?"

I told him, "I'm not sneaky.
I do real honest things.
But if my task could set you free
I'd even wear bear wings."

"Your mission is to sneak up high,
BEWARE of loose, low rafters.
You'll need to keep your head down low
To avoid head-whack disasters!

"Let's synchronize our watches now
To plan when you'll be back!
And if it isn't trouble, friend,
Will you bring me back a snack?"

I asked him, "Tell me, what's a watch?
And what does synchronizing do?"
He said, "I heard that on TV
But, I still don't have a clue!

"I am serious though, about that snack.
Anything you bring I'll love.
And please try not to squish it
While you're climbing up above!"

28

OUR MIDNIGHT ACCOMPLICE

I said, "My roommate Billy Jones
Has licorice jelly beans.
I'll ask if I can have a few.
He keeps them in his jeans!"

Roy said, "Grab more than just a few!
I'm so hungry, I've got splotches!
Now hurry up, be on your way
And, forget about those watches!"

This adventure was so thrilling
I was anxious to begin.
Ms. Flopsy said, "I like him,
He will be just like our kin!"

It was 11:45,
The guards would be out soon.
I tried to walk real casually
Just to get back in my room.

I walked across the wet mopped tiles.
I slid across the floor.
My slide stopped at my private room,
Then I opened up my door.

My creeping wasn't quiet at all.
I was still a clumsy bear.
Billy asked, "Hey, Eli, is that you?
I need to know who's there!"

I told him, "Yes, I'm back now.
I just checked out some noise.
Do you still have all your jelly beans?
I'll take ten in trade for toys."

He said, "They're stuck in one big mass.
They melted in my pants.
They made a very sticky mess.
Now they're covered with red ants!"

I said, "I'll take your whole jeans mess.
I'll deal with those ants later.
Here, take, my favorite squeaky toy.
I must return the favor."

I gave him my duck, Scallywag,
He was a yellow pirate.
He had one patch on his left eye
And he squeaked when folks admired it.

Scallywag was charmingly ruthless.
He would make my bath time fun.
He loved to float in bubble baths
Shouting, 'heave ho' when we were done!

Billy laughed at seeing Scallywag
"Your duck is one great trade!
He is worth more than my jellybeans.
Tell me why you need my aid?"

29

ANTS IN YOUR PANTS!

Billy said, "You're acting strangely!
Please share, what's going on?"
I told him that I had to leave.
It was time to find my home.

He asked, "Right now? Why such a rush?
It's the middle of the night!"
I said, "There is no time to talk.
My time to go is tight!"

"Why do you have to go so fast?
Where will you go from here?
Why do you need my jelly beans?
Did Dora get you cleared?"

"I'll have to send a note to you.
Tonight, I have one chore.
I need to get some things and go.
Can you help me out once more?"

"I'd really like to help you out.
I will go to all extremes.
Please tell me what I need to do
Do you need more than my jeans?"

I told him, "No, just fold your jeans
Into a small, tight square.
I need to know those pesky ants
Cannot escape from there.

"Place your jeans then in a zippered bag
Please, seal it up real tight.
I need to take your jeans and beans
And pray those ants don't bite!"

I quickly climbed up on my bed.
And, grabbed a pillow sack.
I filled it with the things I'd need
To carry on my back.

30

What's in the Sack?

My sack would hold most everything.
I'd put my boots on last.
I'd need to make a smooth escape,
And I'd need to run out fast!

My boots were secret weapons
They would help me jump up high.
I also grabbed my hero's cape,
In case I had to fly!

I scanned the room for other things
I thought that I might need,
But time was short, and midnight rang.
It now was time to leave.

I remembered mother's photo then,
And the special card she'd sent.
I pulled them both down from my shelf.
I refused to get them bent.

I decided that they both belonged
Inside my zippered heart.
So, I pulled the catch down gently
(This would be my brand-new start!)

I also packed Ms. Flops-A-Lot.
I'd need my special friend.
I then got Billy's home address
For my pen-pal notes to send.

Billy offered me a jar of jam
His mom had given him.
He said, "You'll need snacks for your trip."
His eyes began to brim.

I said, "You keep that for yourself.
I forgot I had a jar.
I never thought I'd eat it all,
But my trip might take me far!"

And lastly was the camera
That Dora gave to me
To capture special moments
As I healed from surgery.

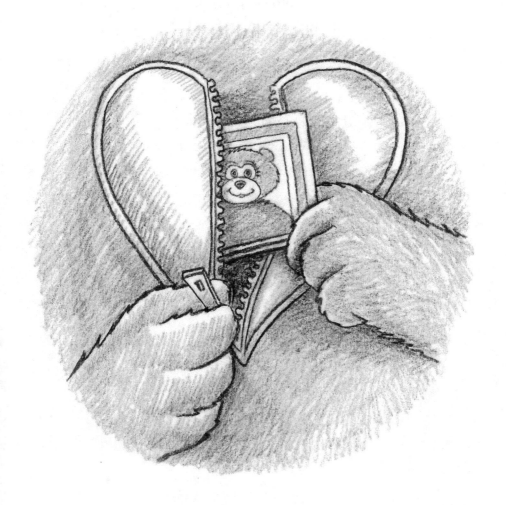

It was an instamatic.
Each photo came out fast.
It only took ten seconds
To have memories that would last.

I then tightened up my hero's cape
And touched my heart's "tattoo."
I slipped into my jumping boots
To begin my great rescue!

31
A Little Help from My Friend!

My rescue started slowly.
My boots kept falling off.
Each time I jumped, one foot came out.
Billy laughed so hard he coughed.

I jumped three times up on the bed.
I rose two feet and yelped!
I needed to get three feet more,
So, I asked for Billy's help.

"Hey, Billy! I could use a lift.
I need to get up higher."
He pulled the brace right off his neck.
It was what I'd require.

I said, "Before I climb this brace,
Let's get a photo please.
I want to capture our great day
One minute now.... say 'CHEESE'!"

I took the photo that emerged
I shook it hard five times
We waited ten more seconds to
Reveal our sneaky crime.

I gave the photo to my friend.
I said, "Mark down this day
That Eli Bear began his quest
To go back home to stay!"

The brace was not too sturdy.
Billy pushed me to the top.
I climbed up on the shaky brace
And I prayed I wouldn't drop!

But the bed was cushioned way too much
The brace just sank right in
We had to get another plan,
Then Billy Jones just grinned.

Billy said, "I have a great idea!"
As he smiled his freckled smirk.
He said, "Give me one minute more!
I know something that might work!"

He ran to grab some beeswax.
He dabbed it in his hair,
He spiked his crew cut nice and firm
Then said, "Now hop up there!"

(Ms. Flopsy said inside the sack,
"You weigh twice as much as him.
You are either going to squish him
Or fall down and bust your chin!")

I climbed his shoulders anyway,
I grabbed his greasy head.
His hair was like a tabletop
With a sturdy patch of red.

So, with one leg on his shoulder
And my free leg on his head,
I pushed up very gently
From my launch-point on my bed.

I made sure Billy was ok
I climbed up carefully,
He said, "You're doing fine up there
My neck's just fine you see."

His flat hair helped me balance.
I pushed off with my boot
I reached the tile above my bed,
As Billy hollered, "SCOOT!"

I pushed the tile and grabbed my sack,
My big butt wiggled through.
I peeked back down at Billy Jones
And gave a big, "THANK YOU!"

It was great to work with Billy Jones
He felt like family.
He helped me out with all he had
Sharing unconditionally.

32

THE LONG CRAWL

I crawled real quietly, inch by inch
Right through the ceiling vent.
The map was where Roy promised.
It was dusty, wet and bent.

I saw the room where Rascal was.
I then heard all the guards.
They were cleaning up the kitchen table.
They had finished playing cards.

Their shift was starting just like mine.
We both were running late.
I had to get to Rascal fast,
A mistake could seal his fate.

Then all at once I had an itch.
Good Lord, those ants were mad!
They ate right through that plastic bag
The bag now...not so glad.

The angry ants were biting me.
Their jaws broke zip-lock seams.
Their tiny breath stunk up the place
They smelled like licorice beans.

I remembered I had brought my jam.
I opened up the jar.
I smeared some on the furnace wall.
Its fragrance spread real far.

The ants all made a perfect line
To eat my jam that night.
They left Roy's licorice jelly beans
And marched straight to their delight!

33

LICORICE ANTS...YUCK!

I heard a rumble down below.
Was it Rascal or his tummy?
The growling sound was fierce and loud
I'd be glad when he said, YUMMY!

I whispered in a low-deep voice,
"Dear Roy, it's time to go!"
I must have scared him half to death.
His breathing got real slow.

He must have thought his angels
Had come to claim his breath.
He shook inside the box and said,
"Oh, please don't take me DEATH!"

He said, "Dear Lord, forgive me
For all those things I stole!
I know I can be better here,
Please, now bless my sneaky soul!"

I laughed so hard I nearly peed.
I had to tell the truth.
"Hey Rascal, it is Eli here.
I'm up here, in the roof!"

He said, "That wasn't funny, kid!
Your voice confused me so.
I need some licorice jelly beans
How 'bout three before we go?"

I said, "Just wait a minute!
I have to get down there.
This landing might get ugly.
I am still an awkward bear."

I took my cape from 'round my neck
And tied it to one rafter.
I climbed down carefully from my perch
To avoid a crash disaster!

He said, "Now untie all these ropes
That bind me in this trap!"
And as I lifted up the box...
He jumped up in my lap.

He looked just like a 'robber cat'.
He had two little hands.
His long white whiskers tickled me.
We had carried out his plans!

He hugged me for a minute
And then he said to me,
"You are my Superhero, friend.
It feels great to be free!"

He ate the beans I gave him.
At first, he did a dance.
And then he spit them on the floor.
"These taste like licorice ants!

"This taste is really nasty!
I have to get it out.
There's one ant stuck here on my tongue.
Can we find the water spout?"

"We don't have time to get a drink.
You'll have to swallow him!
Just make some spit and wash him down.
Now, we must go, my friend!"

He smacked his lips and said, "Let's go!
Add one more place tonight!
The kitchen holds my one desire
Which gives me great delight!"

Rascal showed me how to scale a wall.
It was his "ninja move."
He ran straight at the wall and pushed
His feet up in one groove.

His feet propelled him higher up,
Then he grabbed one ceiling tile.
He pulled up in the rafters,
Looked down at me and smiled.

"Do you think that you can do that?
You'll require both speed and grace."
I ran straight at the stark white wall.
I slipped and smashed my face!

"That's not the grace you needed!
The speed was just okay.
I think you'd do much better
If that wall weren't in your way!"

I got angry at that heartless wall,
So I smashed into the door.
The locks fell off, the door fell down
And collapsed onto the floor.

I said, "Hey Rascal, I've got strength
Even if I don't have grace.
Let's both meet in the kitchen next
To feed my broken face!"

As Rascal climbed above me
I slithered down below.
We both could use one kitchen raid
Before we had to go!

Though our mission wasn't perfect,
We both were on our way.
One final prize was just ahead.
There could be no delay!

34

Hello Honey!

I slithered in the kitchen.
Roy dropped in from up above.
We opened up the fridge's door
To reveal our honey love!

As we filled our sack with jars of jam
Rascal said, "This tale's for you."
He said, "This jam has been around
Since 1932.

"It was created by a bear
Whose name was 'Droopy Drawers'!
He was an easy-going bear
Who spent his life outdoors.

"He lived in ancient caverns
Up in northeast Tennessee.
He loved to chew on bubble gum
And fly around for free.

"He liked to blend great mixtures
Of berries, nuts and honey.
He only made it for his kids.
It was never sold for money.

"They say old Droopy had to take
Ten 'Bees Don't Sting Me Pills'
Each time he made a special batch
Of jam up in those hills.

"When Droopy blew away one day
From blowing giant bubbles,
His kids decided then and there
His mix could solve their troubles.

"They honored him by naming jam
After their sweet Daddy Droop.
They sold jam by the hundreds
And made a lot of loot!

"His treat is loved by everyone
It's sold throughout the land.
And, I can never get enough
Of 'Honey-Beary' Jam!"

"Did you say Honey-Beary Jam?"
I said, "This is a SIGN!
My mom said Father works for them
And has for a long time!

"Give me a jar! Let's check it out!
The label has a clue.
It might provide a street address
Where we'll be guided to!"

The street I found said Copper Springs.
The state was Tennessee.
The town was shown as Bear Ridge.
The address was Three-Three-Three.

I knew then where I had to go
To get close to my home.
With Rascal as my brand-new friend
I wouldn't go alone!

We started packing jars of jam
That we would take with us.
Then, I heard shouting down the hall.
It made an awful fuss!

I peeked outside the kitchen door
And saw an angry man.
He started running straight at me
With an empty garbage can!

35

THE SCARY NIGHT WATCHMAN

The man was with security.
His badge said Morris Gloom.
He said, "I need that raccoon back!
Who let him leave that room?"

The mad-man chased us 'round and 'round.
Roy bit the watchman's leg.
Roy got out with his jars of jam
But left me there to beg!

"I'll get him next!" the madman said,
"But first I'll deal with you!
Why did you help him to escape?
I'll have to punish you!"

I told him we were sorry,
We knew to steal was wrong.
He said, "So, you are in on this?
You're right where you belong!"

His anger seemed to grow and grow.
He was so very mad.
My apology was not enough.
There was nothing I could add!

He turned the trash can upside down
And as he raised his arms,
I pulled the red switch in the room
To engage the fire alarms!

I ran out through the kitchen door
To the sounds of children screaming.
The docs and nurses all ran down
With ten alarms all ringing!

I knew right then I had to leave.
I'd been here now forever.
I had to go find Rascal first.
We'd need to leave together!

36

TIME TO ROAR!

The place was crazy and so loud.
Six firemen all ran in.
The kids and sirens each screamed out.
I had to find my friend!

I then saw Rascal with our bag.
He'd slung it on his back.
He said, "I'm hungry, just a sec!
I need to grab a snack!"

I said, "We have to leave right now!
That mad man's after us!
We need to find a quick way out.
We don't have time to fuss!"

And as I spoke these words to Roy
The angry man was there!
He said, "I've got you both right now.
It's time you say your prayers!"

I then released my first bear roar.
It knocked him to the ground.
We scampered down the long white hall.
Our racing hearts did pound.

Then Rascal got a great idea.
"Let's run back to your room.
Perhaps your roommate, Billy,
Can help stall Morris Gloom."

Roy asked, "Can Billy block the door
With his bed to slow Gloom's chase?
We need some time to hold Gloom off,
That could help us slow his pace!"

Roy's next idea was brilliant!
He said, "Here's what we'll do,
Let's tie your sheets and towels up
Together... two-by-two!"

He said, "We'll tie them to your bed
And through your window drop,
But if your sheets aren't long enough,
Then to the ground we'll plop!"

Poor Billy's bed was built on wheels.
We forgot to lock his brakes.
When Morris Gloom pushed his way in
Billy paid for our mistake!

Billy's bed went flying 'cross the room.
His brace flew in the air.
It landed right on Morris Gloom.
It gave him quite a scare!

Morris saw we both were headed out.
The window was our plan.
We tossed out all our tied-up sheets
Not knowing where we'd land!

We scurried down the linen sheets.
We were only halfway down.
To help us gain more distance
Billy had a small breakdown!

He pretended he was having fits.
He threw his things at Gloom.
He then picked up my squeaky duck
To throw across the room.

Morris stepped on poor ol' Scallywag.
The noise caught him off guard.
Billy left our noisy room in haste
While Morris slipped down hard!

Morris shook himself off quickly.
He saw us slinking down.
He had one chance to get us back
And keep us out of town.

We were 30 feet from touching ground
When we heard an angry cry!
"So, there you are! You foolish boys!
It's time to say goodbye!"

37

CAN I FLY?

Morris grabbed our knotted sheets and pulled
We moved back towards our room.
We had to make a risky choice,
We had to make it soon!

If we let go and tumbled down,
Two stories we would fall.
Or we could let Gloom pull us up
And have a nasty brawl.

Our first choice would take faith and trust
That we would be all right.
The second choice, we'd have to fight
And pray we'd keep our life!

Then, Rascal Roy ran up the sheets
And bit the mad man's hand.
He wanted to protect my life
But that was not my plan!

The mad man leaned out far to grab
Poor Rascal by the tail,
But when he did, poor Morris slipped,
And through the window sailed.

Our sheets came loose, the bed frame slid,
We, too, began to fall.
And I remembered Dora said,
"The Great Bear hears your call."

I opened out my hero's cape
And looked up to the sky.
I then told Roy, "Please, grab my leg...
...We both are going to fly!"

I asked the master of the winds
To send a loving breeze,
To lift us up and set us down,
Real gently, on our knees.

And as I spoke, a breeze arose.
I stretched my cape out wide.
We were lifted up, then floated down,
Delivered side-by-side.

Rascal said, "That ride was magical!
And what a great relief."
He asked me what my secret was,
I told him MY BELIEF!

It was my first experience
In nature's trusting hand.
I had spent my life inside four walls.
Now I was free to roam the land.

I smelled the crisp air of the night,
I heard the cricket's song.
My heart and feet now grounded me.
I knew where I belonged.

Billy leaned out of our window
Saying, "Man, that sure was neat!
Our pal Scallywag held Morris up
So you both could hit the street!"

I then thanked Billy for his help.
I said, "I'll be in touch.
Please say goodbye to Dora.
I will miss you both, so much!

And thanks for sharing Flopsy!
She is the perfect friend.
She's always here to listen
And she lets me play pretend!"

We had but one more thing to do.
We'd do it right away.
I could not leave until I knew
That Gloom would be OK.

38

A BULLY'S FORGIVENESS

Mr. Gloom had landed on the ground.
We ran to him to check,
He landed in a pile of leaves.
We thought he'd broke his neck!

Roy said, "I'm sorry, Mr. Gloom.
I didn't think my bite
Would cause you to fall down so far.
That was a dreadful sight!

"I didn't mean to hurt you.
I thought you meant us harm.
Oh, please, now open up your eyes
We both are so alarmed!"

Then Morris moved his head around.
He felt us standing there.
He heard Roy's plea and felt our pain.
He took deep breaths of air.

His fall had altered him somehow,
He said, "You both came back?
I thought that I was going to die
And feared my head would crack!"

He said, "I'm angry at the world."
He spoke so sheepishly,
"You see, I wasn't mad at you,
My anger was at me!"

He said, "When I was ten years old
My few friends were like me.
We were never very popular,
And, were awkward socially.

"One day as we were playing tag
Mean kids jumped in our way.
The bullies pulled me from my group
While my friends all looked away.

"The bullies shamed me horribly
In front of all my friends.
What hurt me most was not one of them
Came to help me or defend.

"Instead, they all just laughed at me.
They too then called me names.
I felt alone and ostracized.
Inside me something changed.

"I've felt this way for 30 years.
It makes no sense, I know,
But, I'd lost trust in everyone.
I just couldn't let this go.

"My heart no longer trusts itself.
Why am I so afraid?
To let love in and trust myself.
Fear owns me like a slave!"

He then said, "I feel different now.
Inside me, I have changed,
From your return to check on me,
I don't feel so deranged!

"Until just now I didn't see.
I've treated folks like dirt.
I let no one get close to me
So I could not get hurt."

He apologized and made amends
For scaring us so bad.
He said that we were both the first
True friends he'd ever had!

He then gave me his flashlight.
He turned it on for me.
He said, "I think you'll need this
At night to help you see."

I turned the light toward Rascal's eyes.
He froze there in his tracks.
His eyes reflected back at me.
I had shocked him to the max!

He could not move a muscle
Until I moved the light.
Each time it shined he froze in place.
It was a silly sight.

Rascal said, "Eli you're CRAZY!
Don't shine that light on me.
My eyes at night are dilated
And there is no way I can see!"

I told him I was sorry.
I had a lot to learn.
I said, "Your pupils seemed on fire
Which gave me great concern!"

Morris Gloom just sat there smiling.
His new light touched us all.
He said the light is powerful.
It prevents us from most falls.

We then gave Morris Gloom a hug.
We wanted him to know
That we'd be proud to call him friend.
(Forgiveness helped us grow.)

He said, "I hope to see you soon!"
I said, "That just can't be!
I'm in a race to beat deep sleep
And join my family!"

We said goodbye and turned away.
We heard loud sirens blast.
Gloom said, "Head toward that large oak tree!"
I'd never moved so fast!

The nursing staff was all alarmed.
They called the state police.
They told them that I had escaped
And had not been released!

This was my first night in the woods.
I was scared and filled with fear.
I did not know which way to go
With hibernation near.

39

BECOMING A MONSTER!

We both were very lucky
We were in Roy's "stomping ground."
He knew the biggest "secret trees"
To keep us safe and sound.

We scurried up the aging oak.
We'd made our big escape.
We ate some jam and said good night.
I wrapped Roy in my cape.

I pulled Ms. Flopsy from my sack.
Her heart was beating faster.
I said, "We'll take it slower now.
This day felt like disaster!"

As I held Ms. Flopsy quietly
Our hearts then each slowed down.
We listened to the crickets chirp
And the pulsing sounds of town.

We each dozed off to La-La-Land.
Flopsy cooed while Rascal snored.
The excitement of this harried night
In my mind was not ignored.

I tossed and turned, I still felt trapped.
I had a scary dream
That people still were chasing me.
My nightmare was extreme.

And just as I felt all alone
Roy asked, "Are you OK?"
You're saying weird things in your sleep
I am by your side to stay."

We then heard grown men talking.
We could see them far below.
They said, "There must be some reward
To bring him back you know!"

They said, "He can't be far from here,
Plus, he's only just a cub.
We'll wrap him up inside this bag
Perhaps he is in this shrub!"

It was two searchers seeking fame.
They would try to take us back
To be rewarded for their find.
Roy then reached in my sack.

He pulled out Gloomy's flashlight,
He then said, "Follow me!"
We both climbed down the tall oak tree.
Then Roy just smiled at me.

He said, "They think we're helpless.
Just because we both are small.
Now, get in front of this large rock
And raise your arms up tall."

I did what Rascal told me.
I held up both my arms.
He said, "When I say ROAR real loud
These two hunters we'll disarm!

The "brave men" started toward us.
Roy turned his flashlight on,
My shadow made me twelve feet tall
Just before the break of dawn.

I roared like Rascal asked me.
I moved closer to Roy's light.
With each step I got taller,
The men were filled with fright!

They dropped their sack right where they stood.
Roy looked at me with pride.
We made two grown men run away
And one broke down and cried!

We learned then size can fool you.
It's not how big you are,
It's about the will inside you
That can lead you fast and far!

I knew then nightmares offered me
A chance to make new dreams.
That fears can all be chased away
By our light that shines great beams.

Roy and I both retired to sleep
But we giggled half the night.
The sight of tough men running home
Gave our hearts such great delight!

40

RASCAL ROY THE CAMERA BOY

I awoke the next day wiser.
I had new confidence
That I could handle anything.
I no longer felt so tense.

My first night in the woods was great,
This new day had arrived.
As the morning sunshine touched my face
I knew now I could thrive.

Our first day's journey would be filled
With hope and daring drive.
We knew that we could make it home,
We knew that we'd survive.

Roy then said, "We must travel light!"
So I looked through my sack.
I tossed out toys and useless things
That were heavy on my back.

I then pulled out my camera
That Dora gave to me.
I smiled at Roy and said to him.
"I feel so alive and free."

I asked Roy for a favor.
One I knew that he'd enjoy.
I handed him my Fool-A-Roid
Saying, "We need a camera boy!

"This journey will be epic.
We need to document
The things we do, the folks we meet
And the places where we went!"

Roy smiled a cheesy little smile,
And said, "I'll be your man!
I will make a photo album
Of our trip across the land!"

He slung my camera 'round his neck.
He asked if we could pose
For a selfie of our first day out
Before the lenses froze!

I put my very best smile on
While Ms. Flopsy fixed her hair.
Rascal Roy stretched out his hairy arm
For our selfie in the air.

Our photo turned out perfectly.
We all looked really great.
We were anxious to begin our day.
My heart just could not wait.

We looked down from our friendly tree
That held us while we slept.
Our journey was about to start.
Along one branch Roy crept.

Roy said, "I'm looking forward
To this journey with you friend.
This town was never kind to me.
It became a true dead end."

It was Rascal Roy who landed first.
He said, "Be careful, man!
There's a metal box right by the roots
With the words: Newspaper Stand."

As I edged down slowly from that tree
I heard Ol' Rascal say,
"Hey Eli! Is this you I see
Whose face is on display?"

And there I was, as big as day!
My face was in the paper.
The headline there said "MISSING BEAR...
LEADS GREAT ESCAPING CAPER!"

We knew, then, that our path must change.
We'd have to walk through woods.
These city folks might turn us in.
We'd hide as best we could.

Rascal Roy then shrugged his shoulders
Asking, "Which way do we go?"
I said, "I do not know the way,
But we must beat the snow!"

"Why do we have to beat the snow?"
My furry friend did ask.
I told him, "When big flurries come
I fall asleep real fast!

"All bears must sleep when snow comes down.
We sleep a real long time.
I must get home to Mom and Dad.
And then, I'll be just fine."

We had no clue which way to go.
Our journey had begun.
And then a voice inside my head
Said, "Recall your lessons, son."

41

My Magical Vision

I soon recalled the lesson:
How my heart was taught to hear.
I got real quiet and asked myself
"Where do I go from here?"

I closed my eyes and touched my heart
And thought of Copper Springs.
My mom had told me in her song
The joy our home there brings.

My heart had grown more powerful.
I discovered many ways
To let my heart now lead me
On a new path it could blaze.

I added to my practice
A way to feel my dreams.
I felt the love inside my home...
And the call of Copper Springs.

I also learned to see myself
In the home my heart now knew,
My vision was one breath away
To make my dreams come true.

My imagination took me there.
I smelled bacon in the pan.
I saw me walking up to eat
And my dad say, "There's my man!"

I felt my mother hug me.
I heard the gurgling springs.
I saw my bedroom all prepared
And my walls with bear-like things.

My vision showed an ancient cave.
It had a presence there.
She was a brave and loving soul,
Who protected every bear.

She was tall and filled with music
She could be seen for miles.
I heard her whisper: "Princess."
And my soul was filled with smiles.

The thought of music took me back
To the lullaby mom shared.
I heard her soft song once again
And I knew how much she cared.

I asked my heart which way to go.
My listening did not cease,
And then I heard a whisper say,
"Dear Eli, head northeast!"

I heard this loving voice speak out.
It was a part of me.
It was a trusting, calming voice.
I knew it cared for me.

We headed deep into the woods.
Our food supply was low.
I didn't know my north from east.
And, we faced the threat of SNOW!

42

CLUES FROM MOTHER NATURE

I asked Roy if he knew a way
That we could find the north.
He said that trees would give us clues,
Their moss could set our course.

He told me that, "The moss on trees
Grows mostly on one side.
It always faces to the north.
The moss is now our guide!

"And if we watch the sun each day
When we get up to eat,
We'll see the sunrise in the east.
That's where we'll point our feet!

"The moss will take us northward.
The sun will take us east.
We'll have to walk between the two.
We should be close, at least."

We traveled morning, noon and night,
Our tummies growled and roared.
By day we walked, we tripped, we fell.
By night we dreamed and snored.

We had not eaten in three days.
We both grew very weak.
The days grew dark and very cold.
The weather froze our cheeks.

I knew the snow would come real soon.
We had to get home fast.
With frozen paws and sleepy eyes,
I wasn't sure I'd last.

43

FACING HUNGRY WOLVES

That night a cold rain soaked us hard.
It chilled us to the bone.
We really needed food and rest.
We needed to get home!

Then, all at once, not far away,
We heard loud growling sounds.
The noise was headed straight for us.
Our hearts began to pound!

It was a pack of hungry wolves.
They ran in groups of three.
Their eyes were wild, their fangs were sharp.
We sought the tallest tree.

The wolves closed on us quickly.
I saw and felt their breath.
The fast one jumped and snapped at me.
It scared me half to death!

He missed me by a whisker,
But his teeth stuck in my cape.
It jerked me back and turned me 'round.
We now were face-to-face!

But Roy was thinking very fast.
He said, "One moment, please!"
He raised the camera from 'round his neck,
And asked, "Can you say cheese?"

The vain wolf stopped right in his tracks.
He didn't seem annoyed.
Roy posed him for a photo.
Then said, "Smile, it's Fool-A-Roid!

"I'll take your photo, Mr. Wolf,
And leave it here for you.
It develops on the count of ten.
You can count sir, can't you?"

The prideful wolf said, "Yes I can!"
He grinned a toothy smile.
My cape released when Rascal clicked
And, we ran another mile.

As fate would have it, this event
Had turned us all around.
We headed toward another tree
To keep us safe and sound.

We shot up one tall hickory tree.
We climbed and climbed and climbed.
The wolves growled down below us.
We'd left them far behind.

The wolves were very angry.
The fastest one perturbed.
He said he counted up to ten,
But his photo came out blurred!

We laughed so hard we nearly fell.
Roy's thinking saved the day.
The wolves got tired of waiting
And they all just walked away.

We found a large hole in that tree
And we both just climbed right in.
The tree was warm and kept us dry.
Then, we began to grin!

We smiled because fate led us here.
It was the perfect place.
We never would have found it
Were it not for our brave chase.

We also grinned because inside
That tree was filled with nuts.
We both could now just eat and sleep
In Mother Nature's hut!

44

THE VOICE OF FEAR!

That night Roy said that this great trip
Had set his old fears free.
His trust and faith grew day-by-day
By walking next to me.

He said his hunger drove him,
It put him in harm's way.
His taste buds made him pesky.
He was a thief both night and day.

The past kept his mind busy.
He rarely stopped to feel.
He'd let fear run him all his life,
His mind could not be still.

I told Roy that the voice of fear
Was loud from time to time,
But if he could be brave enough,
Then, courage he would find.

I told Ol' Roy just one more thing
That Dora shared with me.
She said that when I needed peace
To lay down by a tree.

She said to me that Mother Earth
Can take away our stress.
Just lie outside and watch the clouds
And let her do the rest!

I sensed that Roy was tired like me.
We both could use a nap.
We lay down in a wooded glen
In a place called Ethel's Gap.

The birds sang us a lullaby,
The bees buzzed us a tune.
The caterpillars crawled on us.
I dreamed I'd be home soon.

That night Ol' Rascal Roy and I
Both stuffed our face with nuts.
We had to beat that dreadful snow
With no ifs, no ands or buts!

45

BEE CAREFUL!

Our journey took us several days.
The moss and sun were guides.
We nibbled on small roots and bugs
While trying to survive.

One day as we both dug for food
Beneath some plants and trees,
We heard a faint, small buzzing noise
And got down on our knees.

We listened hard to find the noise.
My ear went to the ground.
The noise expanded in my ear
Which amplified the sound.

I flicked my ear; the noise fell out.
It tickled me, you see.
It landed softly on my foot.
It was a honey bee!

The little bee was helpless.
He only had one wing.
Roy looked at him and then yelled out,
"Be careful, he might STING!"

I placed the bee upon my paw
And lifted him to see
If I could save this little guy
And help him to fly free.

I knew the early challenge
With my heart had made me brave.
It made me love my life much more
And each precious moment save.

I asked the bee what he was called.
He forgot what his name was.
I smiled at him and he smiled back.
I said, "We'll call you Buzz!"

I told him we were on a trip.
We just had days to go.
The objective was to reach my home
Before the winter snow.

He asked if he could come with us.
He said, "It's hard to fly!
This one wing makes me circle left
No matter how I try!"

I told him, "Hardship spins us out!
We circle round and round
With thoughts that keep us in one place
Or anchored to the ground!

"There's something deep inside us all
That calls on us to soar.
Our hardship makes us strong and wise.
We value life much more!

"So many of us buzz around.
We jump from here to there.
We rarely land to take life in
Or allow our hearts to care!"

My heart then whispered, "Help Buzz out,
Like others did for you."
I had a bright, inspired idea
And knew what I must do.

I asked Buzz, "Can you can come with us?
My plan may help you fly!
You'll have to be real trusting, Buzz!
Are you a trusting guy?"

He said that he'd do anything
To fly and dive and soar.
I said, "We'll need some tree sap first.
For that, we must explore!"

46

BE KIND TO OTHERS!

We found a pine tree in the woods.
We removed its sticky sap.
I held Buzz gently on my paw
And placed Roy in my lap.

Roy seemed to be uncomfortable,
So, we found a nearby stump.
I put Roy's head on my left leg
While that dead tree held his rump.

I said to Rascal, "Just look up!"
"And please, Roy, do not blink.
I need to pluck four eyelashes,
It won't hurt long... I think."

I plucked those lashes from one eye.
He jumped each time I did.
While Buzz laughed every time I plucked
Roy slinked, and blinked and slid.

He wiggled like a wiggle worm
He tried to squirm away,
But we were set on helping Buzz,
I told Roy, "Not today!"

I took the lashes and some sap
And put them all together.
I glued the wing on Buzz's back
So, he could fly forever!

Buzz tried his wings and said great things.
He was overcome with joy.
He thanked us both for saving him
And kissed brave Rascal Roy!

We all proceeded on as one.
We let Buzz lead the way.
We all had sacrificed to see
True love now on display.

47

Look for Signs

The woods grew darker as we hiked.
The trees were getting thick.
The skies turned grey and windy
And we needed food right quick!

I thought about my parents.
Buzz thought about his hive.
Poor Rascal Roy just rubbed his eye
And prayed the swelling died!

I asked each one to make a wish
And hold it in their heart.
We each would walk in silence.
Roy asked, "When should we start?"

"Right Now!" I said to Roy and Buzz.
"What will you place in there?"
Roy said, "I only want to grow
Those missing eyelash hairs!"

"Think bigger! This is powerful.
What dream makes your heart sing?"
Buzz said his wish was granted
When we made his brand-new wing.

I said, "My heart must be at home
With Mom and Dad right now."
And Roy said, "Honey-Beary Jam
Would help me best somehow!"

And just as Roy had closed his mouth
A gentle breeze blew in.
It laid some paper at his feet.
He picked it up and grinned.

The paper was a label.
It had come right off a jar.
It came off Honey-Beary Jam.
It must have traveled far!

"How can this be?" asked Rascal Roy
"I just said what I need!
Then, instantly this just appeared.
Is this a trick on me?"

I told my friends what I had learned
From Dora, weeks ago.
"She said the Great Bear talks in signs
When there's something we must know.

"What we must know is that we're loved
No matter where we are.
This sign is what you needed now
To know love's never far."

Then Rascal got excited.
He said, "There's jam nearby!
And love wants me to have it.
And, I will not ask it why!"

I said, "If we find trash nearby
We must be near a town!
I hope that it is Copper Springs
And that we'll soon be found."

So now with hope restored in us
We knew our dreams were near.
I felt my home just days away.
This feeling was quite clear.

We drifted off to sleep that night.
I slept two hours or so.
I felt a chill and froze in fear...
I woke up in the SNOW!

48

THE BLIZZARD

It must have snowed a lot that night
I could not see the ground.
It still was falling flake by flake.
The snow was all around.

I screamed to Rascal, "Hey, let's go!
We have no time to wait!
We must get home now, quickly Roy,
Before I hibernate!"

I looked for Buzz, but he was gone.
I called him many times.
He must have flown away from us.
His wings had helped him climb.

So, Roy and I set off in haste.
We had to beat the snow.
I could not sleep for three months here.
I knew we had to go!

We travelled miles and miles and miles.
The snow did not let up.
My eyes grew heavy as we walked.
Roy said, "Man, please stay up!"

I told him that I must sit down
For just a breath or two.
He told me, "Eli, please, don't stop!
Our journey is not through!"

Flopsy then perked up quite quickly.
She said, "Eli, hang in there!
Something new and big is blowing in
I can feel it in the air!"

I could not help it... I was so tired.
I had to close my eyes.
But then, I heard the strangest noise.
It took me by surprise!

49

GOOD BEHAVIOUR PAYS

It started as a humming sound,
Which soon became a buzz.
The sky turned dark and all was quiet
As chills ran through my fuzz!

It was a swarm of honey bees!
So thick they filled the sky.
Ol' Roy and I lay down to hide,
To pray they'd pass us by!

Roy said, "We sure could use a dose
Of 'Bees Don't Sting Me Pills'
I wonder if old Droopy Drawers
Had hid some in these hills?"

The bees just hovered over us.
One bee came flying down.
He landed smack dab on my nose
And made familiar sounds.

"Oh, Eli please, don't fall asleep
'Though it's hibernation time!
I knew when that first snowflake fell
I'd need some friends of mine!"

I said, "Hey Buzz, you're back, my friend!
You scared us silly, man!
We had no clue just where you went
But you brought us back a plan."

Buzz said the frost reminded him
Of a quote he thought was good,
About the journey of a man
Who went deep in the woods.

He said, "The woods are lovely,
They are dark and very deep,
But Robert Frost made promises
And went miles before he'd sleep.

"I woke up in the falling snow
And I felt my promise too.
I knew deep sleep could end our trip
And just what I had to do!"

Buzz said, "You've done so much for me.
Our quest couldn't end this way!
So, I flew all night from hive-to-hive
Bringing friends to save your day.

"These bees are all my cousins.
They thought that I was dead.
I told them what you did for me
So, they all buzzed out of bed!"

"How can you save me?" I asked Buzz.
"The snow is coming down!"
He said, "We're going to form a fan
And blow that snow around!"

And then, the bees surrounded us.
Their wings made such a swarm,
It blew away the fallen snow
And kept us safe and warm!

50

A Royal Gift

We travelled underneath bee wings.
We went to their main hive.
Buzz introduced us to their queen.
She was glad that we'd arrived.

She said, "I'd like to honor you
For saving my grandson.
'Buzz' lost a wing defending me.
I thought that he was done!

"Good deeds don't go unnoticed,"
The queen said to us both.
"And cleverness will take you far.
Your hearts are in full growth!

"You're welcome here both day and night.
You see we have a pact
We made with a bear named Droopy Drawers
Three generations back.

"You'll learn about his legend son,
He was a charming man.
He made us promise to watch out
For bear cubs throughout the land.

"The bees for miles all knew him well.
He left us such great lore
But now let's get those bellies filled
And warm you up some more!

"To reward you for your kindness
Which has placed you in our hearts!
I have a special gift for you,
I'd love to now impart."

The queen then pointed toward her vault.
Roy asked, "Will we get money?"
She said, "I'm sharing something more!
It's my special hive of honey!

"We make it fresh here every day.
We ship it to a man
Who turns it to a royal treat
Called Honey-Beary Jam!

"We make it all in six strong walls.
It's honeycomb, you see?
It is our home that nurtures all
And holds our family."

She asked Buzz then to grab us all
A tall, warm glass of milk
To warm our insides and to toast
The strong bond Droopy built.

Roy said, "We've hit the jackpot!
This is sooo much more than money.
I must be in the promised land...
The land of milk and honey!"

Roy then said, "I am starving,
But in respect, I must know more.
About your family and your roots.
Can we sit down on the floor?"

Roy asked her, "Where do bees come from?"
And, "What's the oldest bee?"
The queen looked off into the air
And said, "Now, let me see.

"One hundred million years ago
The first known bee was found.
Her body was preserved in amber
Way down below the ground.

"They found her outside Burma,
In a part of Southeast Asia.
She was preserved most perfectly.
Her name was Anastasia.

"Queen bees teach all their children
That they each have jobs to do.
The children soon live life as one.
It isn't hard to do!

"We each have different talents.
We respect each other's skills.
We care for one another
And live peacefully in these hills.

"Our communication is precise.
Our mission is quite clear.
We pollinate each flower
And make honey with great cheer!"

Her story made us hungrier.
Poor Roy began to drool!
It started as a little drip
And became a messy pool!

Roy said, "I love your stories, Ma'am,
But can you hesitate?
I need to get into your vault.
My tummy just can't wait!"

The queen then grabbed her special key
And placed it in the lock.
She opened up the waxy door
And Rascal was in shock!

The room was filled from wall-to-wall
With golden, thick, rich honey.
And Rascal said, "I think your dad
Must make a lot of money!"

The queen then gave us honeycombs
That dripped her royal treat.
And Rascal Roy just stuffed his mouth
While I went to my seat!

We ate the honey then and there.
It really made our day.
By evening, snow had melted down
Which let us go our way.

Buzz said that he would come with us
To give us more support.
He knew where every hive was now.
He called them honey forts.

Buzz shared with us some special news
Which excited Roy and me.
He said, "We're just two days away
From Bear Ridge, Tennessee!

"Bear Ridge is home to Copper Springs,
I've heard the bees there say.
If you go there, you'll never leave!
It's where all bears sing and play!

"According to my cousin bees
Copper Springs is legendary.
All bear moms there can sing and dance.
They're most extraordinary!

"They say, each dragonfly is named.
Each turtle suns on rocks!
I heard time moves much slower there
Since they've removed the hands from clocks!

"I've always yearned to go there.
This trip we'll take together.
It's high up on my 'bucket list'
I will cherish this forever!"

As we hurried on, my ears were filled
With the sound of my mom's voice.
Her lullaby called me back home.
Her words made me rejoice.

I share one final blessing, son,
My joy for you now sings.
If you feel lost, just touch your heart
And return to Copper Springs.

51
MEET MOTHER NATURE

Before we started back outside
I said, "From Roy and me,
Dear Queen, we thank you for your love
And your hospitality!

"We're blessed you still watch over us.
The bees and bears are one.
Sometimes we get your honey,
And, sometimes we all get stung!

"But I know you make life richer.
I look forward to your treat.
If I always ate just berries
I would feel so incomplete."

The queen sat back then on her throne.
She called on every drone
To guard us as we walked away,
To ensure we got back home.

I wondered if my mom or dad
Ever met Sir Droopy Drawers,
And if they would believe that bees
Had been such great mentors!

Buzz said, "To keep on learning,
We need more education.
I'm pleased to introduce you to
The mother of creation!

"Mother Nature truly loves us all.
Without her, Earth would be
A dark and lonely, lifeless ball,
With nothing much to see.

"She makes the grass. She makes the trees.
She makes the rain and snow.
She can destroy. She feeds us all.
She helps all life here grow."

Then Roy and I felt finally safe.
We'd come to trust ourselves.
As Mother Nature took us in
We felt like nature's elves!

We trusted Mother Nature now.
She met our every need.
She gave us nuts and berries, too,
When it was time to feed.

Mother Nature showed her glory.
We learned so much that day.
She took us to her forest's edge
And sent us on our way.

She gave us each a small acorn
To show that greatness lies
Inside a nut that soon will grow
And stretch up to the skies!

"We both are nuts!" Ol' Rascal said,
"And nuts are meant to grow.
They're not afraid to dig in deep
And push through rocks or snow!

"There's something unique in us all.
It just takes time to see.
We all need love and nurtured growth
To be who we must be."

We stepped out of thick woods that night.
Long meadows we soon found.
The moon was full, the stars all smiled.
We were on the edge of town.

I turned back to see the forest.
We'd spent a long time there.
I entered as a scared young cub
And emerged a wiser bear.

52

Catching Some Zzzz's

That night my mind raced with my heart.
My new life, steps away,
Added so much anticipation
That my mind got in sleep's way.

There was so much now to think about.
I thought of Mom and Dad,
I thought of all the friends I'd made
And the journey we just had.

On this special night of thankfulness
I found it hard to sleep.
So, I called on Buzz to help me out
He asked, "Can you count sheep?"

I said, "I have no idea what sheep are.
Can they hold my eyelids tight?
Are they small enough to sit on me?
Can they help me through the night?"

Buzz said, "Sheep are large and woolly
And their breath at night is bad.
I don't know why I said to count.
It was the best idea I had!"

I said, "Well now, I'm wide awake.
Can you share some extra bees?"
He said, "Of course!" Then they buzzed around
And dropped 4,000 Zzzzzz's.

I had never slept so peacefully,
That sound massaged my heart.
My mind went blank, my eyes shut down,
And then everything went dark!

I woke up the next morning
Refreshed and good as new.
Flopsy said, "We're getting closer now!"
I just heard the call, YOU-HOOOOO?"

She said that word has meaning,
It's from someone who's nearby,
It's a kind of special greeting
A local-yodel kind of cry.

I then lifted Flopsy carefully
And wrapped her in my cape.
We headed off together
To explore a new landscape.

A whistling sound was heard far off.
Buzz said it was a train.
He said this place was "Slippery Town"
Because each day it rained.

I saw the wet town down the hill.
The sunrise made it glisten.
We saw small movements down below.
We all stopped to watch and listen.

It was a busy, bustling town.
The cars all formed one line.
They honked at one another
Just to meet some strange deadline.

I never really understood
Why humans rush to get in line.
The woods have paths you make yourself...
Bears have no wasted time.

To me it's either time to eat
Or time to take a nap.
And sometimes when friends need you most
It is time to search for sap.

I felt my home was getting close.
My heart now beat much faster.
We all had made it through the woods
With great lessons we could master.

53

THE MUSTACHED SALESMAN

We needed final guidance now
To locate Copper Springs.
We were so close, I felt it near.
I wished my heart had wings.

Roy remembered, "We've got labels!
From our Honey-Beary Jam!
Perhaps the address can give us clues
So, we can craft a plan."

He reached for his found label
And placed it in my hand.
I started asking strangers
If they recognized this brand.

Then one kind gentleman said to me.
"Why yes, I know a man!
Just look for Pete, he's down the street.
He is known throughout our land.

"They say old Pete knows every street
And dirt road 'round these parts.
His travels take him far and wide.
He keeps great maps and charts!"

As fate would have it for us all
We found the bear called Pete.
He was at Myrtle's Country Store
To grab a little treat.

Pete was a large, black grizzly bear
Who carried lots of cash.
He was a salesman on the road
And had a thick mustache.

We asked him where he'd recommend
We could find some bears that sing.
Pete smiled and pointed down the road,
"Turn left at Copper Springs!"

"This spring," I asked the man named Pete.
"How will we know this place?"
Then Pete looked off as if in trance,
And joy lit up his face.

"Why Copper Springs is magical!"
Pete twirled his thick mustache.
"It's where bear moms come wash their clothes,
While bear cubs splish and splash!

"There, dragonflies know folks by name.
Each turtle skinny dips!
They shed their shells and swish their tails
While doing cannon flips!

"Oh, Copper Springs just can't be missed!"
Pete smiled with great delight.
"Each bear there learns to sing and dance,
Beneath the full moonlight!

I begged for Pete to tell me more
About the singing bears.
He looked at me quite wistfully,
Then leaned forward on two chairs.

"There's a timeless legend of the springs
About a princess native.
Whose spirit teaches every bear
To sing songs that are creative.

"She once got lost inside the caves
In the hollow mountain streams.
Bears helped her find her way back out.
They went to great extremes.

"To thank the bears for saving her
She promised she would stay,
And help the bears all learn to sing
And hum songs every day!

"She taught all bears in Copper Springs
To sing songs from their heart.
They sing in harmony now as one
And each bear sings their part."

(I imagined mother singing there
With the princess by her side.
YES! I felt it deeply in my soul,
That's the place where we reside!)

"Oh, tell me Pete, which way from here?"
My heart knew Mom was near.
I felt her hum my lullaby.
Her tone was sweet and clear.

"Look for the signs to Bear Ridge, boys!
It's up past Turtle Lakes.
Then, cup your ears and listen for
The sound the spring there makes."

Pete asked Myrtle for a notepad
To draw a simple map.
He drew a heart 'round Copper Springs
Then, smiled and tipped his hat.

Myrtle handed Pete his store receipt
With six roses he requested,
He said, "My wife will love this treat!
Flowers keep our hearts invested."

He said, "I've been gone six long weeks.
I hope she'll understand
How much I miss her everyday
I'm her loving, travelling man!"

We all thanked Pete and took his map
I then got 'goosybumps.'
A part of me felt just like him.
My heart felt great big thumps.

I then asked Pete if he had folks
That lived around these parts.
He said his wife lived down the road
And managed Beary Marts.

Pete said he had been out of state
His travels took him far.
He now was on his way back home
And he carried one cigar.

"I got a message weeks ago
That my wife had birthed our son.
I'm on my way to meet them both,
So sorry, I must run."

Then Buzz and Roy and I set off
For Mom and Daddy's place.
We had a new pep in our step
And big smiles on our face.

Buzz said that he would lead the way.
He'd ask his cousins, too.
We all prepared to buzz through town,
A parade of just a few.

I told Roy, "You will love my mom!
Her voice is very sweet.
She'll first sing us a lullaby
Then she'll make us all a treat."

Roy asked, "Can the order please be changed?
I'll take the singing last.
I believe the saying's 'greet, then eat'
Or, it was last time I asked!"

I loved Roy's strong consistency.
He always put food first.
His tummy was his master,
But I guess it could be worse.

Salesman Pete now gave us focus.
Our heart would guide us in.
The wolves and bees turned us around,
And fate had let us win.

We continued on in lightness
It felt like we had wings.
We'd walked for over 20 days
To now enter Copper Springs.

With Pete's kind-hearted map in hand
We all set off to try,
To find the lovely lady
Who sang "Eli's Lullaby."

54

HOME IS WHERE THE HEART IS

My heart invited my mom's song
To help Pete's loving map.
I felt my mother holding me
While I cuddled in her lap.

Her song is heard both night and day
Near Bear Ridge by the lake
Where turtles climb to sun on rocks
And praise each breath they take.

So, Rascal Roy and I ran fast
To Turtle Lakes to see
If we could hear that lovely song
That my mom sang to me.

Buzz flew ahead to listen.
He was mesmerized by the sound.
Her singing made him so relaxed
He sat down on the ground.

We saw ten dragonflies go by.
They cooled us with their wings.
We heard the rushing, gurgling streams,
Saw cubs playing on their swings.

These were the words from mother's song
That she'd placed within my heart.
My lullaby had brought me home.
We'd no longer be apart!

As Roy and I approached the lake
We, too, could hear the sound,
Which echoed all throughout the Springs.
Then, I knew that I was found.

Way up ahead, I saw my mom,
Reflecting by the shore.
I knew right then that she would hold
My heart for evermore.

My mom looked up and saw me there.
She jumped straight to her feet.
She raced around the water's edge
While my heart skipped a beat.

I handed my sack off to Roy,
So I could run much faster.
I raced with great speed toward my mom,
While my heart was filled with laughter.

And when we met we laughed and cried.
We hugged so hard it hurt.
Our hearts were merged as one that day
(Mine had a growing spurt!)

My mom looked up and gave great thanks
For my return back home.
"Your angels all worked overtime,
You never were alone!"

55

GROWING TALLER INSIDE

Mother's hug allowed my heart to fill,
I had a flash of lessons learned.
Those practices all flowed through me.
Some were given, most were earned.

Like, joy is truly precious.
It's one thing that we must find.
It starts with loving ourselves first,
By being true and kind.

Compassion helps us understand
How other people feel.
Our difference is what makes us great
And lets us each be REAL!

The compassion of my roommate Billy
Brought Ms. Flops-A-Lot to me.
I was touched that he sat by my bed
As he waited patiently.

He sat with me for hours,
Ms. Flopsy sat there too.
They felt my pain from that tough day
Knowing what I was going through.

Officer Gloom was changed by kindness
He didn't think that he was loved.
It's amazing how hurts stay with us
Like being pushed and shoved.

It's little hurts that we build up
That can change our best good nature,
We lose our trust in life itself
Then, one frost becomes a glacier.

Nurse Dora taught me how to serve
And give life my very best.
She said, "Live life authentically
And you'll not be second guessed."

And Buzz proved never giving up
Can help you soar so high.
With fierce determination
You can reach beyond the sky.

The queen bee was so gracious,
Her gratitude, sincere.
I learned kindness is rewarded
From a heart that's filled with cheer.

And, finally there is Rascal...
My heart just has no words.
Friends are the greatest gift we have
They're like wings to every bird.

They help us move more smoothly.
They help us soar and glide.
They hold us when we are at rest.
They are always by our side.

I could have never made this journey
Without my faithful friend.
We faced life's joys and hardships,
We made it to this end.

And when we share our special gifts,
Together, all as one,
The world will be a better place.
Oh! Evolving will be fun!

56

THE SURPRISE!

Then, far off, from a distant hill,
We heard the call... "YOU-HOOOOO!"
To my surprise, I saw the salesman
Running toward us, too!

Ms. Flopsy said, "That's the sound I heard!
Last night inside my dream
It was that local-yodel!
Then her heart began to beam.

I yelled, "Hey Pete! What brings you here?"
He said, "My precious wife!
I've loved her from the day we met.
She is my joy in life!"

My mother then began to cry.
She grabbed my hand to run.
We headed straight to welcome Pete.
She said, "Pete, meet your son!"

My heart stood still there on that hill.
I shed great tears of joy.
My father cried with opened arms
And said, "Come here, dear boy!

"I got the news some weeks ago
That I was now a dad,
And 'though I was so far away
It's the best news I've ever had!"

I told him, "Dad, I must admit,
When you drew that map for me
I saw me in your older face.
You're the man I'd like to be!"

I told him that I knew we'd meet.
The signs were all around.
My guidance had been powerful,
It never let me down!

I said, "This journey challenged me.
My instincts now are tuned.
I've really learned to trust myself.
My heart has healed its wound.

I introduced my new friends first
And asked if they could stay.
My parents said, "They're part of us!
Now, let's be our way."

Roy and Flopsy were elated.
They now had family,
And together we'd share all our days
As the "Trusted Traveling Three."

Brave Buzz then landed on my nose
He thanked me for his wing.
And Rascal showed his eyelash stubs
And said, "It's no big thing!"

We headed home as family
My mom, my dad and me,
With Roy and Flopsy at our side.
They were more than company.

Our neighbors ran to greet us.
They welcomed us back home.
My father lifted me up high.
His joy in me now shown.

57

THE PRINCESS LIVES!

As we turned the corner to our cave.
A monument stood there.
It cast a shadow 50 yards
And touched the clouds up in the air.

She was an Indian princess.
The same one from my dream.
She had a face like Dora
With a kind, angelic beam.

Dad said, "Your family carved this maiden
Five hundred years ago.
She is the guardian of our caves
She protects us as we grow.

"She once was lost in cavern springs.
Her people thought she died.
But our ancestors brought her out,
So she now lives by our side.

"The legend of Forbidden Caves
Will continue through you, son.
Each generation has one bear
Whose stories touch someone.

"The elders said before your birth
That my new child would be
The storyteller of our ways
To connect the world, you'll see.

"They called you *usdi wahuhi*:
Native words for 'Little Owl.'
They said you'd be a wise one.
They said you'd make us proud.

I listened as my father said,
"Natives knew right from the start.
They taught their children all to know:
Our first teacher is our heart.

"Now here's my knife, go carve your name.
There's a place saved just for you.
It's at her base, below her face.
You're a bear whose heart is true.

"You are the keeper of the tales.
Please heed your destined call.
To remind all bears and children, too,
There is magic in us all!"

I carved my name as Dad had asked.
Rascal Roy stood by my side.
Ms. Flopsy smiled and winked at me.
My mom was filled with pride.

I knew the next thing I must write
Was my pen-pal note to Billy
To share with him great stories.
Some were scary, some were silly.

I also made a drawing
Of myself with all my friends.
Then sent it off to Dora
(And our friendship never ends.)

I never could have made it
Without Billy, Buzz and Dora.
They all were blessings in my life
And that's what friends are 'for-a'.

Welcome to Copper Springs

58

Gifts from Our Journey

My dreams had all come true for me.
I felt right from the start
This journey would invite me to
Be guided by my heart!

At long last, I had family!
A mom, a dad, and friends.
My heart had truly opened
To let them each come in.

The quest that Rascal Roy and I
Had taken from its start,
Had brought us all together now
To learn to hear our heart.

My weak heart brought me lessons
I could have never gained,
Unless I took this journey home
To let my new heart reign.

It was my quest to heal and claim
The love for me inside
That built my own heroic heart
That now can't be denied!

My world had changed in many ways.
My new heart was set free
To travel several hundred miles
To find its home in me!

My Mom made me a promise then,
She knew what she must do.
Each night she'd share a bedtime tale
When all our prayers were through.

Each night we snuggled in my bed
We had a 'hugging fest'
With Rascal on my left side
And Ms. Flopsy on my chest.

And when each bedtime tale was done
My mom would hum, so sweet.
My heart would warm and hum along,
This was my bedtime treat.

It was this song that led me home
When Mom sang to the wind.
Now she can sing it right to me...
And I can join right in.

(Sweet Dreams Everybody!)

POSTLOGUE:
YOUR JOURNEY'S GIFT

"Your journey on this planet
Will have twists and turns for you.
They each are meant to help you grow,
And surprise you when you're through!

Each step you take is GLORIOUS!
It reveals a MYSTERY.
That you could not discover
If you refuse your, "Meant to be!"

We all can rise when we fall down
We can't grow when standing by,
The paths that push us off the cliff
Can teach us how to FLY!

I know this may sound crazy,
But I now know this is true.
You do not choose your journey here,
Your journey chooses YOU!

So walk into the mystery.
Pay attention at each turn.
Feel the power of each step you take
To receive each gift you'll earn.

My journey brought me wisdom.
Each fall... a brand-new start.
My courage to live life AWAKE
Opened my HEROIC HEART!"

UPCOMING BEDTIME ADVENTURES FROM THE ELI BEAR SERIES

Each bedtime story my mom shared
Gave me some history,
Of all the relatives in our past
Whose simple lives shaped me.

She said most people go through life
And don't know who they are!
But when you know what makes you, YOU!
You'll shine just like a star.

Mom said one key is know yourself,
Then, to yourself be true
And understand your heritage
'Cause it's all a part of you!

She said there is a virtue
That is placed inside us all.
It will embody who we are
It is our heart's true call.

Her stories captivated me.
Each tale taught me more lessons
About key virtues I must learn.
These were my favorite sessions.

Her funny tales taught me about
My relatives back in time,
Who, in some way, changed history.
Their encounters were divine!

For instance, Grandpaw Droopy Drawers,
Who was not known for his fashion,
Encountered Teddy Roosevelt
Who brought worldwide COMPASSION.

Mom's virtuous tales with relatives
And famous people are
The stories that stay in my heart,
'Though most are quite bizarre!

"Please know that you can change the world
Inside you're such a star.
It starts with living from your heart
And remembering WHO YOU ARE!"

Now that Eli has found his way home what could possibly
happen next? How about eight more books of adventure?

Love, Eli Bear and friends.

Eli Benjamin Bear

THE STORY BEHIND THE STORY

Poet and Civil Rights Activist, Maya Angelou once said, "There is no greater agony than bearing an untold story inside you."

This book and related series have been in me since I was a child of three back in 1958. The stories were being refined and polished in my heart for over 60 years. The 1950s were special times. There were fewer distractions from day-to-day life, less stress, more rituals and we had more quality time with one another.

My happiest memory from early childhood was my nightly bedtime ritual with Mom. Each evening, Mom would talk with me about what was the best and the roughest part of my day. She then made up some crazy rhyming story to make me laugh or read my favorite bedtime story of the week to me. The first story that I recall was "Goldilocks and the Three Bears." I loved that little bear!

When the story was finished, we both would kneel by my bed and say our prayers before I was kissed and tucked into bed safely for the night. Those 30 minutes each evening were the most important and formative moments of my life. I loved Mom's sweet inflective voice and the beautiful cadence and rhythmic intonation with which she shared each story.

When I was three-years-old, Mom bought me a Teddy Bear named, Eli, to watch over me at night. That is when I became an imaginative storyteller too. Each night I would share my stories with my bear, "Eli," and together we would imagine daring adventures for us to conquer.

In 2001, my beloved Mom was diagnosed with the early stages of dementia and by 2012 my childhood storyteller was in the debilitating and final stages of Alzheimer's. All of her treasured memories were leaving her.

Eventually, she required more care than we could give her, and we had to move Mom from her home to an Assisted Living Care Center. I knew she felt afraid and alone, so I bought her a Teddy Bear like the one she had gotten for me so many years ago.

I also went up into the attic of our old home where I found the children's stories that she once read to us. With Mom's bear and me beside her to comfort her, we read our childhood favorite stories to her including: "Henny Penny," "The Three Little Pigs," and "Goldilocks and The Three Bears." It was sad to realize that even though she did not know me anymore, she smiled and mouthed the words to each of these old stories from the remaining vestiges of my childhood days.

Please know that the time spent reading, telling, sharing and discussing stories are memories that will live inside of you and the ones you share your tales and adventures with forever.

May my simple little "Family Time Stories" bless and free the magic of the untold stories in your heart!

ACKNOWLEDGMENTS

This book never would have made it into your life without the wonderful people in my life who have guided, inspired, pushed, and ultimately believed in me.

Thanks to my parents, siblings and my friends in the St. Andrews Community in Columbia, SC for the rich experiences that helped form my early years.

This book had an invisible guiding hand from all of my children, grandchildren, teachers, co-workers, partners, spiritual leaders and life coaches who inspired and supported me when I wanted to give up on this story.

My gratitude especially to Julia O., Michael B., Jose R., Cassandra D., Shad S., Kara Nina, Deima, Patrick C., Lori, Wendy, Stephen, Denise, Dan, Jan, Renee, Lindsay, Jordan, Austin, Shelly, Tess, Autumn, Sue, Soffhea, Betty, Merle, Maggie, Ursula, Maureen, Viki, Bonnie, Yen, Marilyn, my Carpinteria Writer's Group, my Passion Test friends, my Higher Purpose tribe, my Meaning Institute friends & supporters and other loving friends who were placed in my life at exactly the moment that I needed them most (you all know who you are).

About the Author: Hal Price

I am on a mission to save the tradition of family bedtime stories...

As our world speeds up & our families speed by one another, I have a deep and growing concern about our future. We've become too busy to have meaningful discussions or to take the time to share and learn from one another. We all want and need to be heard, understood, and ultimately valued. Perhaps, all of this can start with a 30-minute bedtime ritual with the ones we hold most dear.

My stories are designed to provoke thought, meaningful discussion, and to celebrate life. I am writing this series of books to invite families to discover, share and discuss "the magic of us" and the beauty of life.

As a writer, I am honored that my words and ideas have made me a thought leader for corporations like The Coca-Cola Company and a Five-Time #1 International Best-Selling Author & Global Speaker.

I am the proud father of 3 purpose-driven children, two grandchildren and serve Teddy Bear Cancer Foundation in my "heart time".

To learn more go to: www.halpriceauthor.com

ABOUT THE ILLUSTRATIOR: MICHAEL BAYOUTH

Santa Barbara based artist Michael Bayouth has extensive experience in areas such as graphic design, fine arts, storyboarding, sketching, filmmaking and writing.

Bayouth has worked on the hit TV show *The Office* as a graphic designer, the FOX hit TV show *The Orville* as storyboard artist, and designed the animated Johnny Bananas characters for HBO's *Entourage*.

His in-depth knowledge of typography, graphic design and illustration come from years of working with Disney, Stan Lee and the majors in Hollywood. He is also an author and an award-winning filmmaker. His first novel, *Nine Degrees North*, earned many Five-Star reviews on Amazon. His memoir, *In The Shadows of Giants* depicts his life growing up in a Hollywood home with a not-so-tame stuntman for a father. His award-winning feature was cinéma vérité called, *Take 22*. It earned him a *best feature film* award and *best actor* award for comedian, Rick Overton with three other nominations.

He was schooled at Art Center College of Design. He's the proud father of three grown children, all thriving in creative fields. Currently he creates illustration, branding, and fine art from his loft studio overlooking the Channel Islands in Carpinteria, California. To learn more go to: www.bayouth.com

SUPPORT FOR
TEDDY BEAR CANCER FOUNDATION

Dear Reader,

Heroic Hearts Media is proud to support the families and children of Teddy Bear Cancer Foundation by donating a percentage of the proceeds from the sale of each book to their most worthy cause. Thank you for kind and loving support via your purchase.

TeddyBear
CANCER
FOUNDATION

Pediatric cancer is tragic and unfair.

As long as there is cancer, Teddy Bear Cancer Foundation will continue to be there for families in need.

Parents of patients report that non-medical, out of pocket expenditures are the most troublesome because, unlike medical bills, non-medical costs must be paid immediately and are rarely reimbursed.

Mission Statement: Empowers families living in Santa Barbara, Ventura, and San Luis Obispo counties that have a child with cancer by providing financial, educational, and emotional support.

Teddy Bear Cancer Foundation

3892 State St., Ste. 220 | Santa Barbara, CA 93105

805.962.7466

THANK YOU FOR YOUR HEART'S GIFT
TO THIS SPECIAL CAUSE.

To learn more go to: www.teddybearcancerfoundation.org

"Every day of your life is a page in your story.
May your heart speak volumes about the life you lived."

Hal Price

CPSIA information can be obtained
at www.ICGtesting.com
Printed in the USA
FSHW01n0907100818
51259FS

9 780983 356219